The Cabin In The Woods And Other Short Stories

Matt Shea

"The Cabin in the Woods and Other Short Stories," by Matt Shea. ISBN 978-1-63868-054-3 (softcover); 978-1-63868-055-0 (eBook).

Published 2022 by Virtualbookworm.com Publishing Inc., P.O. Box 9949, College Station, TX 77842, US. ©2022, Matt Shea. All rights reserved. No part of this publication may be reproduced, stored in a retrieval system, or transmitted in any form or by any means, electronic, mechanical, recording or otherwise, without the prior written permission of Matt Shea.

Dedication

This book is dedicated to Reverend Stanley F. Jackowski and his wife of over thirty-eight years, Rebecca.

I was truly blessed when a friend connected me with Stanley. My website needed updating, and Reverend Jackowski's computer wizardry was just what the doctor ordered! On a more personal note, my new friend was certainly a godsend. He was that 'go-to guy' who gave me a better understanding about Jesus. I am proud to say that my passion for writing Christian stories has since escalated, with this present publication serving as testimony.

Thanks, Stan and Rebecca! I do believe that these stories will 'wear well' with your five beautiful daughters, and all eight grandkids!

Your brother, Matt

Truth Family Ministries, Inc.
AKA Stan Jackowski Ministries

Founder
Reverend Stanley F. Jackowski
217-474-9166

New Beginnings Church
www.newbeginningsofhoopeston.com

Another fine job, Stanley!

About Renèe Klause

Renèe has a degree in fine arts and pursued her artistic abilities as a floral designer. Today she still does custom floral work. Renèe also served as a paraeducator for many years.

In her late fifties, she bought a large easel and told herself: "One day I'll use this!" A few years later she joined a local art club and received the support she needed. From there, she has been 'Artist Of The Month' several times!

Renèe enjoys the freedom of abstracts, expressionism, and mixed media. She works mainly with acrylics and watercolor.

Renèe painted the very cover of this book several years ago. She always felt that it would make a great cover for a future Matt Shea book. It turns out that she was right! After all, it became the fifth cover Renèe has done for Matt so far.

Renèe wants everyone to feel free to view her artwork. This includes many paintings that can be seen and purchased on Facebook.

Artistic Xpressions By Renèe Klause

Renèe Klause at one of the many art shows she has entered. This particular one was a fundraiser for the arts in her community. She sold half her pieces that day!

Contents

Synopsis

The stories you're about to read are based on the goodness of Christian faith.

In each setting, whether you are at odds with others in regards to who should inherit what, an honest family man trying to earn better for his family, an innocent boy who could always strike up a friendship with any senior (including the town's only bear), or a teen testing the waters with an elder; let faith be your guide.

It will see you through, each and every time!

Matt Shea

The Cabin in the Woods

Introduction

A CRISP MAPLE LEAF RESTS on top of still water.

In silence, its golden radiance matches the reflection of the surrounding trees—a heavenly spectacle under crystal skies that further served as testimony to one's faith.

The dried-out symbol known for valor and integrity was certainly living up to its image. It seemed to have been called for duty, as if it were a majestic ship from past centuries. The leaf had set sail from the opposite bank to deliver precious cargo: a glistening silver wrapper with a chocolate treat inside!

Six-year-old Becky Lynn Foyer anxiously walked the trail that led to the riverbank. Soon, the child wearing a pink jumpsuit with a matching knitted hat pressed both hands against her face. In awe, little Becky had discovered what she was hoping to find! The brown-haired, blue-eyed girl leaned forward and picked up the piece of candy that was waiting for her.

Gazing across the river, she saw the jubilant face of seven-year-old Jamie Marie Foyer, who was dressed in white. Smiling ear to ear, little Jamie had the gratification of being detected. Immediately, she ran toward the trail that led to her home.

It was obvious to all that each child always dreamed of being the other's sister.

***

It would be fair to describe this neck of the woods as God's Country. After all, it was enriched with undisturbed nature encompassed by a flowing rhythm. On occasion, a gentle breeze would whisper through the wildflowers and rustle the leaves. This was a tranquil land full of grace, where each season welcomed the next.

There was more to this slice of heaven.

Folklore states that the Native American has always regarded this territory as sacred. It was clearly secluded from the tribulations of modern society, as if it were protected. Miles and miles of rugged terrain existed between this land and the asphalt jungles laced with noise and crime. Here, it would be impossible to conceive plans for a housing development or a modern-day facility.

It seemed that an additional blessing was also thrown into the works: The 'Two Brothers River' flowed in front of their homes. The currents were deemed magic on this tribal land. Miraculously, there was a section where nature's most volatile storms could never flood, a phenomenon that started upstream at the fork. It all centered around a mysterious piece of land that split the river like the bow of a ship. When the rainy season hit hard, or snow packs melted, the water level would elevate rapidly. Once it reached a threatening level, the surrounding banks would take over. The excess water would then overflow into streams that would reroute the torrent, thus saving the land it was about to devour.

To make this property even more special, it hosted a log cabin and what appeared to be an old stable behind it. The early American structures were built from the very trees and river rock that surrounded them. This rustic Thomas Kinkade setting took one back in time and was a sight to behold in the wintertime. During those months, it would be encased in snow with friendly smoke rising from the chimney. Cardinals nesting in nearby trees added to the graceful setting.

What made it even more desirable was that it united the extended families on either side of the river. Each property hosted a walking bridge that crossed from their respective sides. Together, they met at the patch of land in the middle where the aging couple resided. This was their grandparents' home; and from there a question arises:

Who gets the cabin when Grandma and Grandpa are no longer with us?

And now our story begins...

Chapter I:
The Early Years

BECKY FOYER MADE A BEELINE straight to the kitchen. There, she found her loving mother wiping down the counters. The child, who was almost out of breath, stood before her and displayed the candy she was gifted.

Thirty-five-year-old Francis Foyer looked at her panting angel. Loving hazel eyes matched the innocent blue eyes looking up. Dropping the damp cloth, she placed her arms around her child and kissed her forehead, saying, "Everybody loves you!" Becky hugged her mother with joy.

Francis Lynn Foyer loved having a family. The slender five-foot-nine woman with shoulder- length auburn hair had her hands full, however. She was a single parent who also had an eight-year-old son named Jacob Michael Foyer. He too had inherited the family trademark of brown hair and blue eyes. Thankfully, there was a silver lining to this fatherless equation. Across the river lived an ideal father figure—a lean, thirty-six-year-old single parent who also had two children of the same age. If Francis could select one man to pick up the slack, it would be this dashing man with blue eyes and short black hair. After all, he was Henry Elliot Foyer, the brotherly love she'd grown up with.

***

Jamie Foyer was sharing a victory hug with her dad. The candy treat had been delivered as planned, and all was well. "You made someone very happy today!" he exclaimed with a tear in his eye.

***

Upstream sat nine-year-old Henry Elliot Foyer II and Jacob Foyer. Together, they shared a fishing spot that seemed to be a page right out of 'The Adventures of Tom Sawyer.' This was where Grandma and Grandpa Foyer lived. A rustic cabin from the 1800s nestled at the fork of the river.

Sixty-two-year-old Chester Mitchel Foyer and his sixty-one-year-old wife, Vyerl Marie always felt that they lived in heaven. They cherished living on the land they were raised on and the sturdy cabin they always knew. High beams from the neighboring trees supported the roof of the two-story structure that boasted four bedrooms. A fireplace made of river rock with a crucifix above the mantle was a reminder of its early American history. Family pictures hung throughout the home that had a woodshed out back and a pole waving the stars and stripes. Above the front door hung an old wooden sign that read: 'The Foyer House.'

This was home for the gray-haired couple who wore bifocals and plaid sweaters. The elders with rich brown eyes and gracious smiles had more to be thankful for. Their front deck faced a mild river that channeled on both sides of their property. Looking to the right, they could see their son's home. To their left was their daughter's.

Later, a trout dinner with all the trimmings would be served in front of the fireplace. A family tradition that was a Thanksgiving all in its own. Such nights included song, laughter, prayer, and passages from the Bible. It was another sacred gathering at the grandparents' cabin, with the kids and grandkids all present. An evening that served as further testimony to their faith.

Chapter II:
Growing Up

A FEW YEARS HAD PASSED.

It took Mother Nature almost no time at all for the children to reach their teens. Becky and her older brother, Jacob, were now fourteen and sixteen. Across the river, Jamie was fifteen and her older sibling, known as 'young Henry,' was seventeen.

Time certainly has a way of changing things, but not always for the better. The future mothers seemed to be doing just fine. Each possessed a remarkable resemblance to the other. It was easy for them to convince the outside world that they were sisters. Everything from their flowing brown hair to their glistening blue eyes made the sell. They also did well in school and often cooked masterpieces for the three households.

It was the brothers where the problem lay. Together they had entered the realm of one-upmanship. It now mattered 'who' caught the biggest fish and which rock was thrown the furthest. Competition had set in.

To make matters worse, they were beginning to cast off into the distant future. In time, each would secretly wonder which one would end up with the grand prize: the cabin that lay between their homes. Even questions about the Lord's existence would soon enter their feeble minds...

***

Henry Elliot Foyer II had sprouted. The young man with wavy brown hair and blue eyes now stood even with his six-foot dad. Sadly, his maturity had taken a different path. He seemed to have withdrawn from the household and spent most of his time alone. There were even times when he contested his dad's advice.

Jacob Foyer was in the same league. He too seemed to have distanced himself from his mom and sister. Telltale signs of contempt toward his childhood friend also began to surface. It appeared that they were no longer fishing buddies. They even stopped sitting next to one another in church. It was apparent that the roller coaster ride of adolescence had gotten out of hand for the boys who could pass as brothers.

In essence, it had become a four-alarm fire.

There was also something peculiar going on behind closed doors. Each seemed to be working on some sort of project in secrecy. On occasion they would be seen on their respective banks, gathering pieces of wood and stones that washed ashore. For whatever reason, these findings soon ended up in their bedrooms.

The first part of this mystery was known. It was the future grandmothers shipping off material to the brothers who'd grown distant from one another. The very currents that shuttled candy throughout their childhood was now on a mission of goodwill.

Growing up, the boys made toy boats, a horseshoe pit, bird feeders, and other ingenious contraptions from the surrounding resources. A continuous labor of love that was to be shared by all. Dried leaves and chunks of driftwood were being implemented once again. The crafty sisters were sending out identical

9

shipments, knowing that the brothers' creative sides would kick in.

It was their hope that the boys would eventually reunite as friends and do more projects together. In the meantime, they remained quiet throughout this campaign It was a given that each brother would create something with his findings.

But what?

Chapter III:
Is There Really A God?

THE PRIZED LOG CABIN had its equal about a mile down the road. It was practically a matching structure from the same era, but with stained glass windows. Church services were alive and well in this part of the woods. The few who lived near and far packed the house every time.

On this particular Sunday, young Henry seemed to stray. He was in attendance, but slightly shook his head as Pastor Donovan spoke. The gracious forty-five-year-old who stood at five foot ten had chosen an interesting topic: signs from our Lord. The man with short red hair and soulful blue eyes electrified the room with his message.

Ironically, the concept of receiving signs from our Creator hit a sore spot with young Henry. Throughout his life, he'd always felt overlooked by the Lord. The lost youth had begun to question if He actually existed. His dad took notice of his son's rolling eyes and did his best to maintain his composure. Later that day, they had a talk.

"Henry, what's gotten into you?" his father asked.

"What are you talking about?" replied the son.

"C'mon!" he fired back. "Are you forgetting who was sitting next to you in church today?"

Young Henry tensed up and stared at the floor. A moment of silence passed as the young man gathered his thoughts. Finally, he looked straight at the breadwinner and shared what was troubling him. "How can there be a God when we pray all the time, and hardly have anything?"

The single parent understood what was said and fired back, "Son, it's all about being grateful for having a glass half-full; and that includes having a roof over your head!" The discussion was over. The bewildered teen went to his room and locked the door.

Henry Elliot Foyer Sr. spent the rest of his day on the back porch with a Bible in hand. Looking over the rolling river, he prayed for his son. "Heavenly Father, please guide us..."

Prayers do get answered.

His cell phone chimed with one Pastor Donovan on the other end. "Good afternoon, brother Henry!" greeted the man of the cloth. It was obvious that the pastor was sharing the same concerns. After their friendly exchange, they compared notes on young Henry's disposition. "He's just a young man taking a time-out," he assured. All of a sudden, an idea popped into the pastor's head. "Hey, I've got an idea..."

The dejected dad was all ears!

"The three of us always loved scouting," he pointed out. "Let's get our backpacks and hit the woods for an overnighter! That will give us plenty of time to set your son straight," he added.

Henry smiled at the idea. He knew that his Eagle Scout would never pass up an opportunity to live in the wilderness. That evening, he knocked on his son's bedroom door. This visit was more amicable than their last.

"What is it, Dad?"

"I just needed to tell you how much I love you," he said.

The interaction had started off on the right foot. "I'm sorry about earlier today," said the teen. "It's just that I've always prayed for signs and never seem to get any."

"Son, they do come *when it's the right time.*"

Young Henry digested what was said and muttered, "I just don't know..."

"You'll be just fine," assured the loving mentor.

The topic eventually changed to camping. The boy perked up, as he was now talking to his Scout Master. The thought of Pastor Donovan accompanying them made him feel a little uncomfortable, but not enough to miss out on a campout.

The stage was set for the three scouts. The plan was to brave the backwoods the following day and have a campfire under the stars. Sister Jamie Marie was not forgotten. Arrangements were made for her to have a sleepover with her friend across the river. This would be an evening that included a trip to town for pizza; with Jacob and the grandparents thrown in!

***

That night, Jacob was confronted by his grandparents. Tactfully, they waited for the girls to be in the next room when they addressed him.

"Is there something wrong between you and Henry?" asked Chester Foyer. "We never see you boys fishing together anymore. You two act as if you don't even know each other when you're in church."

Francis had caught on long ago that the boys had a falling-out. She looked down at her son and waited for his answer. Jacob tensed up and gave a blank stare. Finally, he uttered a few words. "We just don't get along anymore," he said.

"Even in church?" cried out his grandmother.

"Church..." he chuckled under his breath. The boy looked up and said, "So far, none of my prayers have been answered." With a smirk on his face, the Doubting Thomas added vicious bite. "I learned long ago that I was just sending my dreams to something that probably doesn't even exist..."

The three adults were taken aback by those words. "You are going down the wrong path, young man!" said the grandfather as he shook his finger.

"I've never see any signs of His existence," he defended.

"Every day, there are beautiful signs all around us," his mom injected. "Every meal we eat is a gift from our Lord. Sunrises, sunsets, when we make a new friend," she added. "Everything!"

"Look," he replied. "I don't think that those things are from *God*."

Grandma Vyerl had something to say. "His grace isn't always beauty. Sometimes He has to change the course of a river."

"Jacob," said the grandfather in a warm voice. "Let's make the most out of this evening. Tomorrow, you and I can go for a ride. We can hear each other out and get breakfast somewhere."

The teenager always loved outings with his Grandpa Chester. The elder had always been there for him throughout his childhood and was a good listener too. That, along with going out for breakfast, sounded good to him.

"Okay, Grandpa."

Chapter IV:
Intervention From Up Above

THE FOLLOWING MORNING came with a slight breeze and threatening skies. The weather forecast had taken a dramatic turn, with the barometer falling like a rock. It was obvious to all that a heavy dose of rain was on the way.

Chester Foyer took his grandson to the old logging roads that were once alive with woodsmen and heavy equipment. The happy grandfather was proud to share the backyard he had as a child. "There are some ponds out here with great fish," he said. "There are even a few abandoned mines that use to produce gold and silver."

The grandson was having the time of his life! He was with the very man who he'd caught his first fish with. The one who assisted his dad at Scout meetings and taught him how to build a campfire. The two chums reminisced about the many adventures they had shared. In time, the real reason for their road trip came to light. It was to be a spiritual retreat.

"How are you feeling this morning?" asked the granddad.

"Fantastic!" came the reply. "I could live out here for the rest of my life."

"That makes two of us!" came a quick response.

Chester Foyer knew that they were on the same page and switched to the utmost important issue. "Jacob, who do you think made all of this?"

Silence followed as the youth stared down the road. Last night's conversation about the Lord's existence was still fresh in his mind. He especially remembered his grandmother's input and gave his answer. "The same One who could change the course of a river?"

"That's right," replied the mentor. "He has His ways of getting a point across when it's necessary."

Jacob digested what was said as a drop of rain spotted the windshield. Within the next minute a few more fell. Suddenly the dark clouds erupted into a heavy downpour. "Looks like our showers have arrived!" said Grandpa Chester in a jovial tone. Rain was cascading everywhere as puddles formed.

It was always known that this Native American land had a spiritual harmony with the rain. It delivered life through the streams and rivers it fed. It also gave signs from a Higher Power. There were even rains that transformed old paths into newer ones; reaching deeper into the souls who were chosen to witness.

No one knew of this mysterious phenomenon better than grandpa Chester; the guy who lived there his entire life. "Boy, it's really coming down!" he exclaimed. "I wonder if the Lord is trying to tell us something..."

Chester Michael Foyer couldn't have been closer to the truth. The Three Brothers River was already high from recent storms and began to do its *magic*. Various pinch-points began to overflow into streams that now resembled an open fire hydrant. From there, the ravaging flow would spread to other existing channels and eventually meet downstream.

Some of the back roads were already in the process of being washed away, including the one the grandfather was on. Native legend always promised that new passageways would appear in such situations, *for those who believe.* Grandpa Foyer was raised to believe. After all, he had encountered a few challenges in that region where his faith had been tested.

The old-timer saw the fear in his grandson's face. "Just relax and pray, Jacob. We'll be taken care of," he assured.

The dip in the road that lay ahead was now a pond increasing in size. Chester had no choice but to stop. At that moment, a stampede of gushing water several hundred feet ahead was blasting toward them. Its force would easily take the pickup and anything else in the way.

Not far in front of them and to the left came cavalry! It was a massive mudslide carrying large boulders, full-grown trees, and tons of water from an embankment. The avalanche carried enough force to dig deeply into the dirt road; thus creating a trench over twenty feet deep. It carved a new path for the oncoming destruction. The buddies were saved as they watched massive water splash up against the makeshift retaining wall and take a ninety-degree turn!

Jacob was breathing heavily with his mouth wide open. He digested what had just happened and immediately recalled the words his grandmother had shared the day before:
"Sometimes He has to change the course of a river..."

The youth now understood what his grandparents were talking about. Looking to the sky, he started to laugh. Finally, he glanced at his grandpa and said, "I guess the Lord has been with me the whole time..."

***

Moments before that day's rainfall, a hearty breakfast was served at a campfire. "That was good, Dad!" praised the son.

"We need to get your dad in the kitchen more often!" laughed Pastor Donovan. Pastor looked up at the dark clouds and asked, "Do we pack it in, or do we want to move on?"

It took a millisecond for the father-and-son team to answer at the same time: "Move on!" The trio was already packed and ready to go.

"I have an idea," said the pastor. "Let's find a good trail and have our Lord guide us to an ideal place for a morning service."

"Hey," replied Henry Sr. "I like that idea!"

The men looked at young Henry. "I guess that's okay," he said in a soft tone.

Pastor Donovan then gave a group hug and prayed to the Lord to find such a place. A chosen spot where He could lead them to. Once done, he addressed young Henry. "Keep your eyes peeled," he said. "It wouldn't surprise me if God led you right to it."

***

It was apparent that the tension at last night's campfire had subsided a bit. When the two elders attempted to discuss the Lord's goodness, the message seemed to have fallen on deaf ears. It was obvious that the teen who felt overlooked in life had some demons to contend with. Wisely, the grownups changed the subject to past scouting events and fishing trips. The men winked at one another, knowing that the following day could bring new hope.

***

Without wasting any time, the trio began the second leg of their journey. Soon they came across a clearing that had a few trails going in different directions. "It's your call, son," said the dad.

The boy studied his options and selected the one on the far right. "Might as well see where this one goes," he said.

At that moment, young Henry felt a raindrop. Soon a few more sprinkled about, getting the attention of his companions. Within a few minutes, a vicious downpour was underway. The excess from the Two Brothers River quickly made its presence known. Rain water was streaming down the cliffs that surrounded them. A nearby creek was noticeably rising as their trail transformed into mud. Streams began to appear out of nowhere. Instinctively, Junior led the others to higher ground and found another trail that outlined a mountainside.

The rain-swept vegetation caused logs, brush, and rock to slide down the ridge just behind them. Moving forward was now their only chance for escape.

This unfamiliar path eventually took the scouts to a lower elevation, where the danger of rising water and fallen trees awaited. To everyone's surprise, they came across- what appeared to be a logjam. Trees that were uprooted and washed away had become entangled within the gully they now rested in. A closer inspection showed a ray of light glistening through from the other end. A slight cloud break was all it took to guide our heroes.

Young Henry had no choice but to brave the unknown and persevere. He entered the small opening and discovered that the logs were serving as a makeshift tunnel. He took several more steps as the others followed. In awe, they looked around at the canopy *nature* had provided. Suddenly, a spiritual message of great significance caught the eye of one Henry Elliot Foyer II. He spent precious seconds to verify what he was confronted with. Junior then shared his finding. "La, la, loook over there!" he stuttered while pointing.

His dad and Pastor Donovan turned and saw a setting of spiritual beauty. There, standing before them were three massive logs of equal size. They stood upright, with the center one slightly closer. Miraculously, each was leaning against a log placed horizontally, about two feet from their broken tops. The ceiling made of branches, logs, and brush allowed temporary sunlight to cast a beam on each 'cross'. Another ray of light was touching a stump placed 'front and center' that resembled a pulpit. There was also a partial log that had a smaller one of almost identical dimensions two feet in front of it. That too was highlighted by a glimpse of sunlight. It gave the appearance of a bench with a place to kneel. This 'pew' lined up perfectly with the stump.

What young Henry had found was the ideal place of worship they were looking for.

"I'll get out my Bible," said the pastor. The dad and son sat in the pew as Pastor Donovan stood at the pulpit. The service was brief, and soon they continued on the upward trail leading to safety. Once they exited the wooden sanctuary, they turned to look at it one last time. In an instant, the rising waters washed the logjam away, *as if it had never existed.*

Henry Elliot Foyer II became a man that day. He looked directly at the men who'd witnessed what had just happened and said: *"I believe."*

Chapter V:
The Family That Prays Together...

BECKY LYNN FOYER AND HER CROSS-RIVER FRIEND were gathering more pieces of bark, twigs, and pebbles. Another shipment for the brothers was in the making. Meticulously, they compared each item to assure that the boys were still receiving identical material. Together, the future great-grandmothers cast a prayer when each gift was launched in their respective currents.

Within the hour each shipment was discovered. From there, they were immediately taken to a more secure setting behind closed doors.

***

Sunday arrived with sunshine and a much-anticipated event taking place. Grandma Vyerl was turning seventy! The family that went to church every Sunday would celebrate her birthday that afternoon. This milestone would also come with a different spin to it. Earlier that week, the loving grandparents announced that they felt it was time to expose a family secret.

Once church let out, the extended families went to the cabin off the river. They couldn't wait to celebrate Grandma Vyerl's seventieth; and to learn what was about to be revealed. There was also another peculiarity thrown into the mix. Jacob and young Henry each arrived with wrapped gifts. The cousins, who were still not on speaking terms, noticed that each present appeared to be the same size and shape.

In time, all were gathered around the picnic table for the birthday celebration. At the head of the table sat the seventy-year-old guest of honor in all her glory. Amongst the balloons, streamers, and presents were the smiles she'd watched growing up. The family members who had enriched her life with much love and happiness.

Vyerl stood up and thanked everyone for remembering her birthday. She then got down to business. "There is much more to this day than my birthday," she said.

Everyone looked at one another in suspense.

"It's clear to everyone present that we have a blessed family," said the grandmother. "Chester and I decided that it's time to share some of those blessings that took place a very long time ago."

Those listening remained silent.

Grandpa Chester stood up next to her and gazed at his family. Looking at Vyerl he said, "I'll take over." Clearing his voice, he pointed at the front door of the cabin. "Does everyone see that sign above our door?" he asked. Everyone turned toward the door and saw the old wooden sign that read: 'The Foyer House.' Looking at the elder, each acknowledged that they could see it. "That sign used to hang over the old stable behind the cabin," he stated. Chester Michael Foyer paused while trying to find the right words to say. Looking down he gathered up all the courage he could. He then scanned his family and began to speak. What came out of his mouth took the breath away from all present.

"That's because it's wasn't a stable to begin with. It was an orphanage that your grandmother and I were raised in." The trembling old man then concluded what had to be said. "What I'm

23

trying to say is that your grandmother and I were never married. We are actually siblings who were placed in that orphanage because we never knew our real parents."

Everyone stared into a blank space as they absorbed what was said.

Grandma Vyerl began to explain the family history in greater detail. "Chester and I were in diapers when our parents left us on the church steps down the road - and vanished. They must have known that The Foyer House Orphanage was just down the road, and that we would have a home. This cabin was where the staff lived. It was their duty to make sure that we were loved, fed, and kept warm. They washed our clothing and did their best to educate us."

"Maybe they were orphans like us," commented Chester.

"One day, we became the oldest children in The Foyer House," she said. "Chester and I helped look after the younger children, who were just as needy as we were. When the state built a newer facility in the city, we were allowed to stay here and finish out our lives. When that happened, we took on the last name, 'Foyer.' It was our way to thank the Lord for what He had provided us, and to carry on the tradition."

Vyerl had more to explain as she pointed to Henry and Francis. "We made a pact at a young age to adopt another brother-and-sister team who also needed a loving home, like the one we were blessed with."

Francis broke into tears and ran to hug her brother, Henry. He held his sister with the realization that they had entered life the way their adopted parents had.

Chester had more to say. "We didn't want either of you to know this when you were growing up. It was for fear that you might have felt unwanted – as we did growing up."

Several minutes passed without anyone saying a word. Chester and Vyerl looked at their adopted children, knowing that it was their turn to disclose a family secret of their own. In time, they confessed that there was something they needed to tell *their* children. On occasion, each child would ask whatever happened to their other parent. The answers were always somewhat vague and conveniently put on the back burners. Finally, everything was about to come out.

Tactfully, they explained that they, too, felt the compassion to adopt children who were from the same family. This was an idea that was channeled through them years ago. At one time they were volunteers at the orphanage in town. The very one they were adopted out of, unbeknownst to them. It was an eye-opener where they couldn't help but love the needy children they saw every day. What they noticed was that single children were adopted out at a faster rate. It was the siblings who were getting the short end of the stick. Usually they were the ones left behind, or split up into different homes to have a life never knowing one another.

"Today's institutions kept better records on which unwanted children were siblings and in the same boat," said Henry Sr. Young Henry, Jacob, Jamie, and Becky were assured that they were all born into the same family. Sadly, they were the victims of parents who couldn't handle life's hardships and became dependent on vices.

"We loved the four of you so much that we took all of you!" explained Francis.

"We thought that it was for the best to raise you within two homes that were not far apart," explained Henry Sr. "We were never married to anyone before; but that wasn't going to stop us from being a family with what we had to work with. We purposely had one boy and one girl in each home because of our limited situation. We wanted each of you to have the security of 'one' home instead of wondering who you should be living with, or where..."

"It was important to us that the four of you would be loved and brought up together," added the adoptive mother. "It was also our plan to tell you everything when everyone was old enough."

The children with matching brown hair and blue eyes looked at one another with tears in their eyes. Nothing needed to be said. Instinctively, they got up and embraced each other for a lengthy time. After a while Chester Foyer spoke up. "Hey," he cried out. "This is supposed to be a birthday party, and we have some gifts to open up!" The presents were placed in front of the birthday girl, and the festivities began.

A beautiful forest green sweater was from Francis. She had knitted it herself. "Oh, this is just lovely!" exclaimed Vyerl.

Henry Sr. pointed to the deck facing the dividing river. A beautiful wooden bench that would seat Grandma and Grandpa quite comfortably rested there. Their boy had made it himself. "Oh, we're just going to love it!" she commented.

Together, Becky and Jamie presented their gift. Vyerl unwrapped a bird feeder that was painted red. "Oh, my cardinals will be so happy with this!" she cried out.

Chester handed an envelope to his sister. It held a simple card that stated how much he loved her. "Well, I love you too!" came her response as she kissed his cheek.

It was now time for the grand finale. All were staring at the almost identical wrapped presents. The ones that peaked everyone's curiosity, including young Henry and Jacob.

Jacob's was opened first. Vyerl's jaw dropped when she discovered it to be a greatly detailed model of the cabin that she and her brother lived in. "Oh my word..." she said under her breath.

Next, young Henry's gift was opened. To everyone's surprise, it too was a detailed model of the very same cabin. That is, with one exception: Each teen had done the side that faced their home; with the other side exposing the inside of the cabin. *Their side.*

Each boy looked at the other in dismay. *They wondered how on earth did the other come up with the same idea?*

It was then that further spiritual intervention came into play. Without any thought, the seventy-year-old joined the two halves together. The wooden floors, stairwell, fireplace, and shake roof all interlocked perfectly. Young Henry and Jacob looked at the finished product and knew it was the currents that brought them the materials in the first place. From there, the idea of what they were to create was channeled during the process. They realized that making these models wasn't their idea at all. It was just like the signs given when one was led to a temporary altar, and the other saw the course of a river change. At that moment, each knew that the family cabin wasn't a prize to fight over. It was a gift to be shared.

There was something even more important. Each now knew that they had a brother who was always there the whole time. Someone they always had to play with. That God-given life that they loved, fought, and learned from.

"Well, I think it's time to start cooking our meal," suggested Vyerl.

"We could sure use some trout to sweeten the pot," Chester wisely suggested.

It was like old times, with young Henry and Jacob casting their lines into the water. Immediately, Jacob got a bite. "I'll get the net!" cried out young Henry.

Today was positively the best day in the lives of the Foyer family. The changing of events had blessed everyone that afternoon. This especially held true for the future great-great- grandmothers. The girls looked at one another with an angelic grace that could only come from our Lord. They now knew that something they had always prayed for and felt deep inside held true:

They really were sisters.

The End

George

Introduction

PAYDAY HAD ARRIVED WITH FORTY-ONE-YEAR-OLD George Willis Freeman knowing what to do. The accountant, who stood at six feet even had already calculated which fires to put out, and which bills to address later.

The mild-mannered, heavyset man with short brown hair and matching eyes scratched his head. It was obvious that his financial woes were not going away anytime soon. True, he always met his monthly expenses, but the American dream of getting ahead just seemed to elude him. The former high school football star grimaced with the realization that he still had one oar in the water.

Fortunately, there was a silver lining.

George's quarterly bonus arrived on time. In fact, it was none other than Benjamin Miles Tucker IV himself who personally handed it to the loyal employee. The 'Big Guy' who only spoke in brief sentences and never smiled. "A good day to you, Freeman," he said with direct eye contact.

George never quite knew how to interpret the owner of the company. The lean, gray figure with thinning hair seemed out of place. This dignified entrepreneur, who only wore suits accompanied by wire-rimmed glasses from last century, always seemed to be a bit tense. It was as if something was wrong with the short, introverted man...

31

It was the paychecks and bonuses that George did understand. His slightly 'above average' wage that would be enhanced by a mere pittance every three months, *if standards were met*. Such gifts were secretly declared personal play money.

Foolishly, the extra dollars would be channeled toward an act of desperation. Initially, the married man with two children would waste it on buying worthless lottery tickets. Then there were the frivolous purchases. Used items purchased in thrift stores that were meant to be sold for profit on the internet - *if there were any buyers.*

In time, he would embark to what many considered to be the dark side of town. A no-man's land where stories of small fortunes arriving at the snap of a finger circulated.

And now, our story begins...

Chapter I

IT WAS A TRANQUIL EVENING with the Freeman household gathered around the dinner table. George beamed with pride as he fixed his eyes on each child.

There was his fourteen-year-old daughter, Mary Jane (who was already having boys calling her). The honor student, who was a star volleyball player, had inherited some of her mother's traits. She was a classy auburn haired beauty with chestnut eyes. No one could argue that it looked like she was ready for Hollywood.

Sitting next to Mary was her big brother, George Jr. This product of manhood was definitely a carbon copy of his father, plus an extra two inches! His matching stature, along with his determination and relentless drive, equated to football scholarship offers in the making. *Little George,* as he was affectionately referred to, also had brown hair and matching eyes. Most importantly, the sixteen-year-old possessed a compassionate soul like his father.

George bantered back and forth with his children as dinner was being prepared. Questions about school and their interests were discussed. Soon a warm meal was served, with the woman of the house receiving an ovation, followed by a group hug.

In this family, *everyone* was important.

Forty-two-year-old Crystal Jane Freeman was Mother of the Year material. A beautiful five-foot-seven-inch auburn-haired woman with chestnut eyes who religiously stayed in shape. She was the mom that every local kid knew and was heavily involved with the community. Crystal was the greatest blessing one George Willis Freeman had ever received.

This particular evening came with a special ring to it. It was to be somewhat of a family free-for-all night at the Freeman household. Crystal and the kids would each have some friends over, with dad meeting up with the guys in his church group.

***

After dinner, George volunteered himself to do the dishes. Mary Jane and Junior cleared the table. Soon the breadwinner of the house was hugging his family with kisses thrown in for the wife and daughter. "And dinner was fantastic!" he proclaimed. George then put on his coat and opened the front door. "Bye!" he called out as he entered the night.

***

George Freeman loved Wednesday evenings. After all, it was the best of both worlds. It gave him quality time with his family and then carried over to his weekly brotherhood. A fun night out with the guys while paying homage to the Lord.

***

George was soon sitting in front of a roaring fire surrounded by friends. With a Bible in one hand, and a cider in the other, the second part of his evening was now underway. Such affairs always started out with the men forming a circle while holding hands. Together, they would bow their heads and say The Lord's Prayer. Once seated, a member would randomly quote a favorite verse from the Good Book. Immediately, each would share the personal message they felt through those heavenly words.

Occasionally, a tap on the shoulder would come from a friend who just arrived. Discussions ranging from our Creator's goodness, to cute family stories or personal problems, were all a part of Wednesday nights.

In time the occupants of the room would naturally drift into smaller groups. This was to accommodate those who wanted to play billiards and shuffleboard, while others played chess or found themselves in a card game. There were also those who just simply wanted to huddle together for a good conversation laced with laughter and amusing stories. It was within this close-knit group of friends that George's life would change forever.

Clark Johnson, Rudy Vancil, and Jim Renolds were in true form that evening. They, along with George and his neighbor, Lance Wadsworth, seemed to be having the most fun. Intense laughter pulsated between stories, creating a laughing session that echoed throughout the hall. This rotation of court jesters and standup comics could have sold tickets.

The rhythm of humor began to slow down when Pastor Kerns approached the group. "Nice to have you guys with us tonight!" he greeted.

Each responded with "Good evening, Pastor," followed by a warm handshake.

It was always known that the Pastor made his rounds throughout the hall with a collection basket for all to see. Wallets immediately opened and pockets drained when it was time to donate. George's generosity was no exception. In fact, he always tithed ten percent of his earnings every month. Cheerfully, he placed a twenty-dollar bill into the basket. A *much-needed* twenty-dollar bill. "Thank you, brother George!" said Pastor Kerns.

"It's my pleasure, Pastor," came his response.

Clark, Rudy, and Jim all followed suit with friendly exchanges made.

Lance then gave a handsome donation while doing his best to not draw any attention. The alert Pastor was attentive however, and saw the hundred-dollar bills placed in the basket. The spiritual leader's eyes bulged in approval as he looked directly at Lance. "You have certainly been generous lately!"

George saw the sizable donation and heard the Pastor's comment. The man who was struggling with financial woes wanted to hear what Lance had to say. In a humble tone, he gave his response. "The Valley Casino has been good to me lately."

A seed had just been planted.

Chapter II

GEORGE GOT VERY LITTLE SLEEP THAT NIGHT.

In silence, he would think about his neighbor, Lance Henry Wadsworth. The tall, lanky, blue- eyed, brown-haired, harmless specimen with buck teeth. A man who would never pass as a being of 'higher intelligence' and worked in a used car lot. The forty-one-year-old who would have been a perfect extra on Green Acres. The guy who was always smiling

George did have to give his happy-go-lucky neighbor some credit, however. He knew the man had dignity and would never lean on anything that suggested a handout.

There was more.

Lance Wadsworth did have his own home, and his two teenagers were a good influence on George's own children. Lance's wife also donated time to the community. The one-car family was apparently surviving well enough.

Regardless, a thought kept racing through George's mind:

"If a guy like Lance could do well in a casino..."

***

Hours later, the diligent CPA was at the office juggling numbers and finding loopholes. It was practically like being at home. After all, everything he learned in his profession was also applied on the home front.

Resourceful ways to improve utility bills and curb family outings had all been subtly implemented without raising a red flag. Grocery shopping for the best deals and finding the cheapest gas in town were all part of the equation. Stretching the almighty dollar - *just like at work.*

George definitely had a battle on both fronts. The irony was that the corporation he worked for was doing just fine. It was his family's financial matters that were hanging in the balance.

The conservative accountant who brown-bagged it every day was still scratching his head as he looked for answers. Such times were known to have a few prayers thrown in. A time-out in life to reach out to our Lord and ask for guidance. Whenever a disparity consumed George Freeman, he would reflect back on the most recent visit he had at church. That place where God Himself presents all the answers one would ever need.

The fellowship he attended the night before was still playing in his mind. The many Bible verses that were shared continued to give great inspiration. At times he caught himself chuckling over some of the humorous stories he'd heard. Thoughts of those who attended last night brought a smile to his face. Then memories of his neighbor, Lance surfaced. The guy who donated a wad of casino money to help fortify our Lord's kingdom.

George had heard many stories about casinos; both good and bad. The man of faith always assumed that it was best to play it safe and stay away from them. To many, gambling was considered a taboo. Some had even declared it sacrilegious.

But was it really? He'd just watched a brother give generously to the very house they worshiped in. A large sum of cash acquired from the casino across town. George decided to take the long way home that day. He would drive by the casino to see what everyone was talking about.

***

The well-advertised Valley Casino was easy to find. Attractive billboards with television-like footage led the way. Beautiful people sharing the excitement of winning and tantalizing meals being served in luxurious settings presented itself to the traffic it faced. In minutes, George could see the famed multicolored fountains spraying high into the air. Behind this cascading phenomenon was a golden light show spelling out the name: 'The Valley Casino'.

The enormous, stately structure outlined with gold, brass, and swirling festive lights called out to all. It would be impossible for anyone not to notice this spectacle. To some, it would rival seeing the Land of Oz for the first time. For others, it could be what a child would expect if one was to follow Santa back to the North Pole.

This sensation put George Freeman into a momentary trance. For the first time in his life, he felt like a multimillionaire with class!

***

While driving home, George noticed his neighbor, Lance. He appeared to be all alone as he entered a café. Without hesitation, George parked next to Lance's car and entered the diner. "Well, hello, stranger!" called out his neighbor. "Hey, if you have the time, why don't you have dinner with me?"

The offer was music to George's ears. It was an ideal time to pick his friend's brain and learn more about the casino he frequented. "That sounds great!" exclaimed George. "I'll have to check in with the boss first."

"I understand," commented Lance.

George pulled out his phone and dialed. "Honey, I just ran into Lance and we decided to have an early dinner together; if that's alright with you."

"How wonderful!" she exclaimed. "You guys have fun, and send Lance my best. Love you!"

"Love you too!" replied George.

The professional accountant was now in his element. He would systematically pump some information about the gold mine Lance Wadsworth had discovered. All of this while enjoying a meal with a friend who he considered to be *a little too naive to sense ulterior motive.*

Greed had set in with George Willis Freeman.

Once dinner was served, George opened fire. "You sure seem to be getting your share of blessings lately."

"I most certainly have," agreed Lance. "I can only thank our Lord for His favor," he added.

The seasoned numbers man digested the testimonial that he just heard. It appeared that the nicest, most humble person he'd ever met in his life didn't view gambling as being *wrong*. In fact, it seemed to be a partnership formed with our Creator Himself!

This premature conclusion put George's conscience at ease. Questions were now being asked about the casino. "Tell me, Lance. What's it like in there?"

"It's like a palace that anyone can go to," he said. "They're always open with tons of people and lots of money floating around."

George was sold and wanted to hear more.

"They have a coffee shop and five restaurants, including a real nice steakhouse. A guy can go there any time of day or night and have a cup of coffee with pie," he pointed out. "Trust me," he emphasized. "Their food is the absolute very-best ever!" Lance took a bite of his sandwich and continued. "They even have a few shops, and the cheapest gas in town is right there!" he added. "The casino is incredibly beautiful, inside and out. Everybody is happy there."

Lance pulled out his wallet and said, "Look!" He displayed what looked like a credit card with 'The Valley Casino' printed on it. "This is my player's card. It gives me all sorts of discounts once I'm inside. Meals, the gift shop, shows, and even when I buy gas!"

George leaned close to the card in admiration. "Does that include playing their machines?" he asked.

"Absolutely!" responded Lance. "You need a card to play, but you get bonus points when you play. Those points add up to free meals, gifts, and extra gambling money - as long as you're playing there."

George wanted in. "How much does one cost?" he asked.

"They're free!" exclaimed Lance. "All you have to do is to introduce yourself to the front desk and they'll take care of you. They even gift all new players some free gambling money to get started."

This was all good news, but George wanted to know his secret about having so much extra cash in his pocket. "Do people ever win money at those places?" he asked.

"Some do," he responded. His neighbor seemed to be getting a little reluctant at that point. He appeared to be shying away from George's advancing interest. "That place is basically a city all in its own," said Lance. "They even have live shows and concerts."

The struggling family man reversed course. With assertiveness, he looked directly at his friend and asked if any of the slot machines were known to pay out large sums of money. "They're all known to do that," responded Lance in a disappointed tone. "It basically depends on how much a person is willing to gamble, and if they're lucky..."

George smirked with the belief that his neighbor was trying to hide something. He would take one more shot, and then abort his mission. "Tell me," he asked in a soft tone while leaning forward. "Are there any specific slots that seem to do better than the others?"

Lance leaned back with his hands clasped behind his head. "Some seem to be more popular than others," he pointed out. Then he rattled off a few that always seemed to be played. Lastly, he mentioned one final machine that seemed to have customers always lined up. "The Twilight Galaxy has been a real popular one lately."

George interpreted that as an insider's tip. It was as if Lance was a stockbroker from Wall Street who'd just given him a midnight call. George leaned back in his chair and gave a warm smile. He winked at Lance and said, "Thanks."

Chapter III

GEORGE RETURNED HOME FULL OF DREAMS. He even stopped by the store and bought his better half fresh flowers.

"For me?" exclaimed Crystal in astonishment.

"Yes, for you," came the reply as he hugged and kissed his wife.

"What's the occasion?" she asked.

"I have this incredible family to come home to every night. That's why!" he answered.

"How was your dinner with Lance?"

"Great!" he said. "I really appreciate that guy." Next, the proud family man knocked on Mary Jane's bedroom door.

"How's my princess doing?" he asked.

"Fine," she responded. "But now I'm even better!" A warm hug ensued.

"That's what I like to hear!" responded the father.

George Jr. was in the hallway and spoke up. "Hey, dad, we missed you at the dinner table."

"Well, I missed you too; but it's not over yet," came his reply. "I think we all deserve to go out and have some ice cream! When you two are finished with your homework, we'll go."

"Wow! Thanks, Dad," exclaimed Mary Jane.

"Cool!" said Junior.

Within an hour, the family was in town enjoying their tasty treat. What was more important was that they were enjoying each other. Reports about school life circulated. Crystal talked about the Woman's Group she had recently joined and how much she enjoyed it. George kept his end up and mentioned his Wednesday fellowship. George Freeman was a happy man that evening. He was living his idea of the good life. Little outings with the family that would soon occur more frequently.

After all, *he would be coming into some money soon...*

***

George was in his office when he took notice of a calendar. It hung on the wall next to his coat rack. The theme picture for the present month was one of a hot, glistening muscle car from the '70s. Polished chrome wheels and rally stripes accented the sexy machine. It was the very car he'd wanted in high school. The one he secretly still wanted. It reminded him of the casino he'd driven by the day before. The showpiece that mesmerized him matched the same class that the casino did. *It also held the same dreams.*

Looking around his mundane workspace, depression set in. It dawned on him that his earning power had hit a dead end years ago. He felt like a rat trapped in a maze of outdated furniture and filing cabinets. A cruel and unusual dilemma for a hard-working man who wanted the best for his family.

His working world also had a mystery attached to it. His boss, 'The Big Man', Mr. Tucker, Benjamin Miles Tucker IV, always seemed off in a world all his own. Many business associates had pointed out that he never smiled. On one occasion, George brought an entire room down when asked about it.

"I once thought about trying to make him laugh, but I was afraid his face would crack."

Why is he that way? George asked himself.

Chapter IV

THE WEEKEND HAD ARRIVED for the Freeman household. It was Friday night, and the festivities were about to begin! The family would attend Junior's basketball game, followed by a well-deserved pizzafest at Cesar's Pizzeria.

Mary Jane and her mom had plans for Saturday. The girls had an appointment at a hair salon with a lunch to follow. This was to be a mother/daughter outing that might even have a movie thrown in.

Junior would tackle the yard, and then meet up with his friends later.

George would get up early to make pancakes and brew fresh coffee. Fried eggs with juice and bacon would also be waiting for the family. He would then relish some valuable alone time and go for a walk.

The night would finish out with the stunning beauties cooking up a surprise!

Sunday was always the Freemans' most important day of the week. It was their day to pay homage to and serve the Lord. This particular Sunday would go the extra mile. George's fellowship would stay after church services and welcome a local drug and addiction program.

This was how George first met his neighbor, Lance Wadsworth. A few years ago Lance was troubled with life, along with a few vices thrown in. It was at such a gathering when the frail stranger with buck teeth introduced himself to the congregation. He reached out and gave himself to the Lord and wanted to join that church. This kind of procedure interwoven with an addict on the mend, required a sponsor.

It was none other than George Willis Freeman himself who immediately volunteered.

"I'm so happy that I found this place!" exclaimed their newest member.

"We're all happy," replied George. "Especially the Lord!"

"I feel like I just won a contest," cried Lance.

"You did!" responded the sponsor, who was now affectionately holding his brother's shoulders. "It's a *happiness contest,* and we're all winning!"

Lance Henry Wadsworth would carry those words for the rest of his life.

George listened to Lance's story when he gave testimony. Among other things, he knew that the man desperately needed money. That very night, George gave what he could to the stranger he believed in.

There were other acts of charity that George and the fellowship provided. It was common for them to drop by a struggling household to deliver food and pay their utility bills. There were nights when George received a late-night phone call in distress. Times when he got out of bed to get someone who was stranded on the road. Sometimes it was to play the role of a designated driver and bring a lost soul who had wandered into a gin mill home safely.

This adoption blossomed into a success story with a lifelong friendship in the making. From there, it was Lance accepting others who were walking the path he once did. Many times another lost soul got off the street and committed their life to our Savior. All because they could relate to Lance. *He was once there himself...*

It became common practice for the humble servant who worked on used cars to extend himself to others less fortunate. Just as George had done for him.

***

Monday started off with George reviewing the books.

This was what he considered to be a special perk. He was trusted to know where every penny came from and where it went. It also showed how much each employee got paid.

It was there in black and white that Benjamin Miles Tucker IV was more than just fair to his employees. He consistently shared windfalls by issuing all an unexpected bonus check. When the company took a hit, the paychecks kept coming.

The businessman from another era kept a steady beat and never missed a day of work. He was greatly respected by all who knew him.

Still, the CEO was a bit of a sourpuss. He would attempt to socialize the best he could at the company's Christmas parties and summer barbeques. Brief efforts to acknowledge his employees in front of their families was followed by a stiff grin that never showed any teeth.

The twenty-year employee periodically looked at the high-performance chick magnet pictured on his calendar. It was a ride that he calculated a good night at the casino could buy. He then thought about the owner of the company sharing some laughs with someone. *Anyone.* The controller began to calculate what it would take to accomplish that feat. After some thought he reached a conclusion:

A guy would have to win the lottery to pull that one off...

Chapter V

GEORGE NOTICED A TEXT MESSAGE minutes before leaving the office. It was sent an hour ago from his wife, Crystal. It stated how her sister had dropped by unannounced and wanted to take her and the kids out for burgers. It was a spur of the moment idea that they jumped on.

The impromptu message finished with:

"Looks like you'll have the evening to yourself. Love you!"

George had absolutely no plans that evening. He could only view it as the perfect opportunity to venture into The Valley Casino and put his best foot forward. He made it home, took a quick shower and got something to eat.

***

It seemed that in no time at all George was parked at the new casino. Determined, he was ready to challenge the gold mine awaiting. The man on a mission slowly got out of his vehicle and closed the door. Next, he looked up and saw the magnificent empire that stood before him.

George froze in awe.

The commoner's senses were overtaken by the palace of magic lights and invigorating rhythms. Poised and ready for battle, the multimillionaire with class left his shiny '70s muscle car and marched forward.

George approached a well-lit walkway lined by black railings. It was somewhat of a winding route graced with flowers, shrubs, bushes, and an occasional 'Alice In Wonderland' bridge over a creek. This was The Valley Casino's red carpet treatment for their prized guests. It was for the George Freemans who finally found their way to this would-be Never Never Land. A path of hope that could possibly solve all their problems. To all newcomers these streets were paved with gold.

George delicately walked the trail that swayed through the mystical forest. It was the nurturing strings accompanied with horns and the dancing Aurora Borealis filtering through the trees that beckoned him to proceed with his journey.   Moments later, he found himself in a clearing.

His path led to a spotless circular lot meant for valet parking and limousines. In the center was a gargantuan fountain spraying upwards as it gyrated against an array of pastel colors. It seemed to be dancing to music fit for angels. Beyond the fountain, limos, and benches was the main entrance. This would prove to be the pinnacle of this elaborate showcase.

The main entrance was a sight to behold. The structure, which could hold more than the average shopping mall, was also far more inviting. Not only did it maintain the stellar beauty known throughout the entire building; it also bolstered Roman-era pillars that supported the ceiling overhead. Beautiful floral displays with their fragrances further enticed guests to enter this lavish kingdom. Brass hand rails led to the magnificent double glass doors, outlined with more brass. They were masterpieces that stood ten feet high.

To make one feel even more important, uniformed doormen were always standing at their post. It was customary for their answer to the Queen's Guards at Buckingham Palace to tip their hats with a smile. *They* would open the majestic doors for *you*. Cheerfully, all were wished a good evening!

George liked what he saw and felt compelled to march forward. Soon he was being acknowledged by the prestigious gatekeepers, who exhibited the utmost respect with direct eye contact. A message of goodwill was delivered as hats were tipped.

"Good evening, sir!" greeted one servant. "We're so glad that you could be with us tonight."

"Please enjoy your evening, and let us know if we can do anything for you!" said the other.

At once, the gleaming smiles open the matching doors evenly. This was The Valley Casino's way of letting George Willis Freeman know that he wasn't just *anybody*. He was important and deeply respected.

Suspense mounted as the land of milk and honey awaited. A few steps later, he was gobsmacked by a city that only Hollywood could create. What initially got his attention was the nurturing music that carried a certain fullness. That, along with the masses of beautiful people scattered about, tantalized him to explore further.

He was now encompassed by an infinity of oak beams, crystal chandeliers, Tiffany lamps, marble pillars, and exotic carpeting. Looking around, he noticed brilliant water fountains resembling Christmas trees, dancing flame pits where many sat, etched mirrors, and an array of breathtaking paintings and sculptures for all to see.

It was at that moment when a charming voice called out to him. Turning around, George was startled to see a dignified man smiling at him. He was dressed in a black suit with a diagonal red sash over his white shirt. It was as if he were a Grand Marshall for a major event. The stranger extended his hand and introduced himself. "Good evening, my name is Lloyd Bernstein. This seems to be your first time here, and I wanted to welcome you!"

George loved having someone who was obviously in a high position take the fight to him. He responded with a firm handshake and replied, "George Freeman, at your service!" Laughter ensued, with the two engaging in a friendly conversation. They briefly shared where each came from, tidbits about their families, past and present occupations, and most importantly; predictions on upcoming sporting events.

"Hey," said the goodwill ambassador. "Are you aware of the free drinks around here?"

"Free drinks?" questioned George.

"That's right!" answered Lloyd. "You are at The Valley Casino. We have coffee and soda stations scattered everywhere. Always feel free to get a drink whenever you want to. It's on us!" Finally, George's new friend guided him to the counter where he could get his all-important game card.

"I appreciate you, Lloyd!"

"The pleasure's mine. Great to meet you, George!"

The line at the gold and silver Welcome Center had eight tellers and moved swiftly. When it was George's turn, he was overwhelmed by how pleasant the teller was. The attractive woman in her thirties welcomed him and asked for his driver's license. It was like going to the Department of Motor Vehicles. He got his picture taken, and within moments, he was congratulated for becoming The Valley Casino's newest member.

The good news continued: He was informed that five dollars were added on his card for gambling, *and* that he was to touch a screen that would spin the diagram of a wheel with numbers. Whatever figure it stopped at would represent additional gambling cash to be added to his card. George was game and pressed the screen. At once, the multicolor wheel spun into a blur, until it began to slow down. Slowly it came to a stop.

"Congratulations, George!" exclaimed the teller. "You just won an additional twenty-five dollars!"

Within minutes, the newest member was admiring the smiling face on his player's card. He beamed with pride as he looked up at the midnight blue ceiling with twinkling stars. The accountant also liked the idea of starting off his gambling career with thirty dollars of *their* playing money. Most of all, he liked being called by his first name.

George Willis Freeman was now somebody!

He felt like a poverty-stricken immigrant who just arrived in America. The nine-to-five peasant would now wander around this land of opportunity where droves had made fortunes.

While walking his unorthodox path, he happened across an Italian restaurant. It possessed an old world charm resembling a sidewalk cafe in Venice. George studied the candle-lit white tablecloth settings. Authentic pasta dishes with traditional salads and bread sticks were being served. It was all enclosed within a rustic iron corral. The violins made one's trip to Italy complete

Not far away was a festive Mexican restaurant. It too played the happy tunes from their native country. Happy customers could be seen savoring the family recipes laced with salsa and guacamole.

Next he discovered a popular Chinese restaurant. It carried all the charms of past dynasties and had a gracious maître d' in traditional attire.

Drawing its share of attention was a dining establishment that had a vintage silver Jaguar refitted as a salad bar. This place had a few fireplaces and served hearty dishes, including award-winning barbequed ribs.

George then came across a food court. This was where the most popular fast food chains were well-represented. Everything from burgers, fries, and shakes; to tacos, fish and chips, and subs were there for anyone's liking.

George continued his trek and meandered toward the south end of the building. Things suddenly changed.

He was now walking on a cobblestone path that was illuminated by pulsating flames from noble streetlamps. This theme sent George back in time to jolly old England in the 1800s. Sure enough, he could hear the sounds of a horse trotting. Coming into view was a horse and carriage being guided by a stately elder wearing a neck scarf and top hat.

This ride was offered to guests who stayed at the hotel. It traveled through a wondrous forest behind the resort that had trees, brush, stone bridges, a brook, and meadows. Acres and acres of an enchanted Camelot nestled within the seclusion of nature.

George marveled at the regal hotel that faced him. The twelve-story brick building with stained glass stood dignified. Huge potted plants outlined the steps leading to the front door with brass highlights. He stepped on the emerald green carpeting that led the way.

Once inside, he was greeted by a receptionist. "Good evening, may I help you?" George explained that he was greatly impressed from what he saw and wanted to look around. The sixty-three-year-old employee fully understood and granted permission. "We have many who drop by just to look," she said in a pleasant tone. "I'd also like to mention that our members with playing cards are eligible to win a free stay."

That was music to George's ears!

The lobby he was standing in had a glamorous chandelier hanging from a gold chain. The high ceilings with white stucco walls had oak molding. The window curtains were of an emerald green that matched the carpeting. Antique wooden benches and matching leather chairs graced the lobby and hallways. Oak tables with Tiffany lamps and beautiful artwork highlighted the surroundings.

On the first floor, he found yet another restaurant that matched the decor of the lobby. He was able to peek inside a room and saw a kitchen and bathroom made of marble, with every appliance imaginable. A lavish living room with a fireplace and a private lanai with a Jacuzzi were also featured. Beautiful works of art were displayed about. The middle class citizen had no idea that such luxury had ever existed.

He soon left the hotel and embarked to the mainstream of the casino. In his travels, he saw a display of a vintage Harley Davidson alongside a classic 1965 Corvette with a pearl paint job. A sign was displayed announcing that all players with a player's card were in the drawing to win one of them. *These were the toys that George Freeman wanted!* He spent a good twenty minutes inspecting the prized collectables from all sides. The teenager came out in George. He found it hard to walk away.

Moments later, he saw an elaborate display of gold and silver ornaments in a black setting. It outlined a tunnel that led to a golden elevator. Next to it stood an operator in a three-piece suit. A light purple neon sign above the inviting display read *Chamber's*. George had heard of the famed restaurant before. It was to be one of most elite, prestigious restaurants in the entire state. The newbie on a self-guided tour walked the red carpet through the tunnel to see what he could see. The operator greeted him at once and asked if he had reservations.

"Well, no," said the man in a bowling shirt. "I just couldn't help myself. This place is so incredibly beautiful!" he commented.

"Would you like to take a peek upstairs?" asked the operator.

"Who, me?" asked George. "I'd love to!"

The golden capsule opened as the two men entered. It was polished black inside with gold and silver highlights. Harp music from the heavens could be heard with gentle ivory keys in sync. The smooth flight was brief. Almost immediately, the door opened a second time. They had reached their destination, with George stepping into yet another dimension of unequaled surroundings. He was now standing in a dark waiting area lit by saltwater aquariums of various geometric shapes. Beautiful dark velvet furniture with matching coffee tables were for those who were about to have the best meal of their lives. The harps and soft keys upheld their grace.

The elevator operator addressed the host. It was obvious that they had been friends for quite a while. "Do you mind if my friend takes a quick look around?"

"Oh, not at all!" came a cheerful reply.

George entered the room where the patrons who arrived in limousines dined. Saltwater tanks graced the room, with smoked glass tables and candles. The angel strings still played, with a piano softly following. The shimmering gold and silver ornaments and highlights carried throughout.

There was one more feature. The entire back wall was a breathtaking panorama view of the city, including a mountain range. At night, it was a spectacle to behold.

The servers were the best in the business. They delivered the tantalizing gourmet dishes with their personal touch. Their guests who wore fine jewelry and expensive clothing couldn't have been more satisfied.

George left the restaurant undetected. What he needed now was to find somewhere to sit and digest what he had just experienced. He was soon downstairs, sitting in front of a fire pit enjoying a hot cup of coffee. Gazing at the colorful flames, he reflected on all the beautiful people he had met that day. The clerks, receptionists, elevator operator, doormen, and hosts who extended themselves and *remembered his name*.

He thought about the vintage Harley and Corvette that he had a chance at winning. Classics that compared to the dream car on his calendar. The hotel he'd briefly toured that one could live in for the rest of their life. It was possible that his family could have a free stay there! Fantastic restaurants that were full of happy families. The all-around beauty and symphonic waves that carried everyone.

Where have I been? George asked himself.

The man on a tight budget pulled out his game card and admired how personal it was. It seemed to be a deed that verified he had advanced in life. He felt that he was now a member of the most prominent society this town had ever had. It had also gifted him thirty dollars to get the ball rolling.

Motivated, George Willis Freeman knew it was time to stake his claim...

Chapter VI

GEORGE HAD SEEN JUST ABOUT EVERYTHING the casino had to offer - except for what he actually came for. While taking another sip, a woman's voice startled him. "Can I get you a refill?" the employee asked.

George turned and looked at yet another attractive woman wearing a name tag. "That would be wonderful, Patty!" he replied. "By the way; where are the slots?" he asked.

Patty gave simple instructions while pointing.
"Thanks!" came his reply. In moments, a warm cup of coffee was delivered with the new member going tit for tat. He generously volleyed back and tipped a five-dollar bill.

"Why, thank you," acknowledged the host. "Good luck out there!"

***

George finished his coffee and got up to attend business. Soon he was at the top of a stairwell looking down at the city buzzing with every color imaginable.

Multicolored lights that blinked, flashed, spun, danced, and walked harmonized throughout this land of dreams. Trumpets that drew everyone's attention would occasionally sound off. The jingle-jangle of bells would chime. Buzzers, whistles, and alarms were making winners known. Famous rock songs and country-western hits cried out to their fans. Steam, lasers, glitter, and strobe lights beckoned to those who were looking to make a fast buck.

Countless tables with rolling dice, cards, and chips were intermingled in the sea of electronic one-armed bandits. A rolling current of alcohol, wishful thinking, and losers.

The future plutocrat was on deck. Surveying the frenzy below, he pondered where to start. *It just seems to go on forever and ever,* he thought to himself. It was then when another host addressed him. "Can I help you?" asked a charming woman wearing a name tag.

George remembered his mission and asked about the machine that Lance had mentioned. "Yes," he answered. "Would you know where The Twilight Galaxy is?"

"Oh, that's a popular one!" she said. Pointing to the masses below, she gave directions. "If you walk down the main aisle in front of us, it's about halfway down to your right. There's an entire row of them; you can't miss them," she added. "They are greenish with a radio-like antenna that has red Saturn-like rings around it. It's about three feet high and has a silver star on top that flashes. If you walk down a little further, you'll see more to your left."

"Thanks, Sharon," responded George.

"You're very welcome!" came a cheerful reply. "Good luck!"

George began his descent to the floor below. Soon he was in the mix of fellow members chasing the same dream. A swirling flow of desperate souls who were in search of either a jackpot, or the nearest ATM. The losers of society who were always short before payday.

The happily married man and father of two was now standing at ground zero. This was the dark side of town, where the harsh reality of gambling was about to introduce itself. From the outside looking in, it was the glitter of Hollywood and all its dazzle that drew the crowds. Once inside, everything changed. It was now about the human element and their antics.

George cautiously walked down the aisle that swayed with the oncoming masses. At times, he had to stop and turn sideways to give the right of way to what seemed to be a stampede in the making. The congestion was continuous and often resembled a can of sardines.

At times he would step aside and watch the courtship between man and machine. He saw what appeared to be a seemingly innocent-looking female employ her gimmicks. Polished fingernails delivering affectionate strokes while sitting at close range. Seductive eye contact while mastering the art of 'soft talking' to their automated sugar daddy.

He saw grown men sitting straight up and verbally addressing their animated business partner. Choice words could be heard in warm tones graced with compliments as such negotiations took place.

Other stations had become volatile, as if the subject had caught a loved one stealing from them red-handed.

There were those who seemed to be plea bargaining. It was as if they were in court, begging in front of a judge to get a lighter sentence.

Sometimes a patron would jump up and down, screaming in ecstasy. It resembled a dad watching his kid sliding into home plate.

George noticed the machines that had green antennas with radiant silver stars. Turning into the fabled row, he saw what must have been at least forty Twilight Galaxy gaming machines facing each other. Each seat seemed to be taken as a single-file line slowly shuffled through looking for their turn.

George found his place in line and watched the theatrics at play. Tender hands were seen caressing the plastic molds in front of them. Soft kisses touched the glass screen that exposed a rich world of fantasy. Index fingers pointed angrily at betrayal. Some raised their hands up with joy as the pot kept filling.

In time, George was in the other neighborhood with the glistening silver stars - and got lucky! Inches in front of him, a dejected patron slid back to throw in the towel. As the mumbling middle-aged man got up to lick his wounds, the crafty accountant grabbed the backrest and slid in.

The black leather padded seat with a high wraparound backrest was comfortable. It also adjusted to the contours of the forty-one-year-old's mildly overweight body. It held him in a secure position as he grabbed the sides of the coin-operated machine and rolled forward.
George inspected the cockpit he was sitting in and marveled at the controls. He studied the pulsating screen in the center that appeared to be a portal to the heavens. It seemed to breathe life, as if it were taken from the ocean's depths while looking beyond our solar system.

It was an infinity of wonderment.

The new member of the casino pulled out his magic card and inserted it into the adventure that awaited. Immediately, the green space traveler came to life! Various shades of green lit up as the red rings on the antenna blinked. The silver star began to glow as a Star Trek nuclear propellant sound engulfed the area.

George was touched to see that he was welcomed aboard by his first name. It was by an alien-type stewardess (who was rather sexy). In digital print, his gambling options were presented. The humanoid could bet anywhere between ten cents and five dollars. The cosmic gambler had already plotted out his course and vowed to limit his gambling to only fifty cents per game.

Armed with sixty shots, he was ready for takeoff!

The Twilight Galaxy resembled a simulator that took its passenger through the Milky Way and beyond. It would then approach a series of images ranging from the planet Saturn, to Flash Gordon himself. It was a typical slot machine setup that rolled an odometer/checkerboard-like set of images. In essence, it equated to the randomness of a dice game. George would have sixty attempts to see what could become of a four-bit bet.

He struck out on his first six attempts. On his seventh challenge, he connected with three images of the *Lost in Space* robot that triggered a 1960s recording of the famous mechanical star going ballistic: *"Danger, Will Robinson! Danger!"* Immediately, a thundering meteor shower took place with golden coins falling from the stratosphere. George had won $2.50!

Several spins later, he rolled four Neil Armstrongs. At once the national anthem came alive with the immortal words being played:

That's one small step for man, one giant leap for mankind.

Another thunderous meteor shower took place with more gold coins showering from above. George was on a roll and netted $12.75! He rolled the dice another eleven times and finally made another $2.00 by bringing up the planet Earth. Three minutes later, his flight was over.

George was stunned to find that such an exhilarating ride had ended all too soon. True, he did win $17.25 in a short period of time and had fun doing it. The reality was that if it was his money to begin with; he would have failed his family by throwing away $12.75.

It was now his time to leave. While getting out of the seat, another set of greedy hands had already clenched onto the backrest. George was no longer taking notice of the beauty that surrounded him. Instead, he was like a dog with its tail between its legs. Deep inside, *he knew better*.

The man who had just made some pocket change would now leave the famous casino by walking a different path. It was as if he were in hiding. Approaching the main door, he noticed a quaint coffee shop. Looking inside, he saw none other than Lance Wadsworth himself sitting alone in the back section. Counting a fist full of cash!

That guy's not telling me everything, George thought to himself. The first-time gambler left undetected.

Chapter VII

GUILT HAD SET IN FOR THE CHRISTIAN who went to the other side of town. He wrestled with himself on the way home, trying to justify what he had just experienced.

George was surprised to see that he'd beaten his family home. Once inside, he sat down and glanced at the many pictures facing him. Practically all were of his family expressing the joy they had being together. Christmas, Thanksgiving, birthdays, vacations, along with other milestones surrounded him. It occurred that *they* were the reason why he secretively challenged gambling in the first place.

He then took notice of the crucifix in the dining room. It seemed to be drawing his attention, as if it were carrying a message. It was at that very moment when it hit George:

There was only one thing he could do at that point to make things right. He entered the bedroom of each child and put $5.00 in their piggy banks. Next, he put the same amount into his wife's money drawer. The remainder would serve as a fair tithe for church. It would surpass the traditional ten percent *with a prayer attached*.

Mission was complete! Just then the front door opened. "How was your evening, dear?" asked his wife.

"Just fine," he answered.

***

Sunday arrived with the Freeman family attending their weekly services. Once again, Pastor Kerns gave an inspiring sermon. The good man covered many Bible stories that carried a specific message: *Sometimes it's the rich man who needs to call out for help.* The pastor emphasized how our Lord worked in mysterious ways. He stressed that there are times when it's the very charity cases that we give to, that become the ones we have to lean on during hard times. "Sometimes the strong need help from the weak," he preached.

George felt enlightened hearing those words.

When the collection basket was passed around, he dropped his usual twenty dollars along with the remaining balance from his recent gambling escapade. George Willis Freeman immediately felt a weight lift off his shoulders. He was free!

It was then when his curiosity got the better of him. He glanced over to Lance Wadsworth. He watched the grease monkey inconspicuously donate a sealed tithing envelope that was obviously stuffed to capacity. Pastor Kerns kept the secret by nonchalantly giving a wink to the humble servant. George didn't need to ask him where the excess money came from. He already knew.

***

George Freeman was in typical fashion and arrived early to the office. This gave him time to enjoy a fresh cup of coffee and reflect on the past weekend. A lot had happened since he left last Friday. What stood out most was the message that Pastor Kerns delivered. His sermon about rich people sometimes needing help from the less fortunate continued to play in his mind.

His thoughts were interrupted when Mr. Tucker entered the room and gave his generic greeting. "Good morning, Freeman."

"Good morning, Mr. Tucker."

"Freeman," called out the old man, who seemed to tremble. "I'm afraid that I have some bad news."

George sat back and gave his undivided attention. In a sincere tone, the disgruntled elder from another era began to explain himself. George's gut feeling was two steps ahead as he prepared for the worst. "Our business has been victimized by modern technology," he stated.

George could see where this conversation was going and knew he was out of a job. After hearing how hard he'd tried to keep the ship afloat, his suspicions were confirmed. "You're a good man, Freeman," said Benjamin Miles Tucker IV. "I can honestly say that you were the best employee Tucker and Associates ever had." The broken man handed a white envelope to the former employee. "Here is your severance pay," he said with direct eye contact. "It also includes next year's Christmas bonus. I'm sorry, Freeman."

His twenty-year tenure had come to an abrupt end. It was finalized with the formality of a cold handshake. "You might as well clean out your desk and go," were his parting words. With dignity, the failed entrepreneur stood tall and left the room.

George Willis Freeman leaned back in his chair to let things settle in. His mind kept wandering back to Pastor Kern's message. About how sometimes the strong need help from the weak. It was at that moment when the unemployed father of two lowered his head and prayed for guidance.

Chapter VIII

THE UNEMPLOYED MAN SPENT THE FIRST PART OF HIS DAY at the bank. He deposited his sizable check and paid off all his bills. Next, he addressed the unemployment office and got himself into their system. Mathematically, the responsible breadwinner now had months of survival money to coast on. Still, finding a suitable job to see his children through and glide into retirement was his first priority.

George would spend the rest of his day driving around in La-La Land, thinking about his current state. Wondering how he would continue to support his family without causing any panic on the home front. Soon, the elegance of the Valley Casino came into view. Driving past the immaculate parking lot, he spotted the unmistakable faded red Ford Escort of Lance Wadsworth. 'That guy' who had recently discovered a gold mine. Without any thought, George pulled in and soon found himself in the very coffee shop where he had recently spied on his neighbor.

George was pleased to see that his 'friend of lesser intelligence' was sitting alone in a booth. This time, he made his presence known. "Is that you, Lance?" he called out in a merry voice.

Lance was happy to see George and replied, "Well howdy, stranger! Pull up a chair and let's have a meal together." The timing was right for the man who was out of work. George Freeman got the formalities out of the way and quickly addressed his interest.

"You seem to cash in around here," he said.

"The Lord has blessed me from the moment I set foot in this place," replied Lance in a humble tone. It was then that George heard what he wanted to hear. "The moment I got here, my luck changed," he revealed. "When those pennies from heaven started to arrive, I could only think of my friend, George."

Those very comments were the reason why George was there in the first place. The bonding continued over a warm meal laced with small talk. On occasion, Lance would make mention of how much he brought home on a good night. It was all music to George's ears!

Finally, Lance looked directly at his friend and said, "I'd like to share something with you, if you don't mind."

"Sure," came his eager reply.

"My wife and kids are going to be out tonight," said Lance. "Why don't you drop by my place around seven? I want to let you in on something."

"I'll be there!" said George with a wink.

***

George had a wonderful family time that evening. Dinner was delicious and full of intimacy. He shared himself at the table while keeping the dismal news about his job a secret. Even his wife didn't know about it. It was understood that he would be with Lance later that evening. "You guys have fun tonight," said his wife after kissing him on the cheek.

Soon George was in Lance Wadsworth's home enjoying a cup of tea. "So good to have you here!" exclaimed the host. After a while, Lance reminded himself why he'd invited his neighbor over.

"Oh!" he said. "There was something that I wanted to show you. Close your eyes when I tell you to," he instructed. Lance placed his tea cup on the coffee table that faced him. He then got up and left the room. George remained seated as the suspense started to mount. Within three minutes, Lance called out from a closed door. "Close your eyes!"

"They're closed," George answered back.

In a moment, Lance gave his second command. "Now open them."

As soon as George opened his eyes, Lance cried out, "Ta-da!"

George was now looking at his fellowship brother posing in a classic chauffeur's uniform with his arms stretched out. It was as if he were a professional model on the runway. The colors, name tag, and logo on the left shoulder could only have meant one thing: that Lance Henry Wadsworth was gainfully employed at The Valley Casino. In fact, he was wearing the outfit only worn by their prestigious drivers and bellhops.

George was taken as he looked back at the smiling face that stood before him. Lance looked like a page out of Hollywood. "So that's how you do it!" exclaimed George. "I thought that you were making a mint on those machines in there."

"I stay away from them," said Lance. "I'd rather give my money to the Lord then hand it over to those slots." George understood exactly what he was talking about and nodded back in approval.

Questions would now be asked.

"Did you quit your job at the car lot?"

"Well, not exactly," he answered while looking at the floor. "They have slowed down a bit, so I looked at the want ads and saw that the casino was hiring." Looking at George he continued. "My boss was great about it! He encouraged me to get in with them and told me that I can always service a few cars if I ever needed the income."

"How much do they pay you there?" asked George. Lance admitted that it was just a slice above minimum wage. "Is *that* all?" he asked in astonishment.

"Their benefits are the absolute best!" he defended. "They also feed us and give out bonuses. The people there are very nice to me, and I love the customers too."

George cut to the chase and addressed the money issue. "Brother, lately it's been obvious that you've gotten quite a stash from there."

"Oh," replied Lance. "You must be referring to *this*. Lance turned and pointed at a five-dollar bill framed on the wall. George got up and studied the perfectly centered bill in the black frame.

A tear trickled down Lances face as he told the story of the commemorated currency. "That's my first tip," he explained. "The person who handed that to me was grateful because I was nice to them." George returned to his chair and sat down. "A machine could never do what a real person can," he pointed out. Looking directly at George he elaborated further. "The appreciation and respect I feel whenever anyone tips me goes way beyond what any jackpot could ever pay. It doesn't matter how much I get," he added. "It's knowing *why* I got anything that matters..."

George digested what was said as silence fell across the room. Looking at Lance, he could only marvel at his fellowship brother and smile in agreement. It all made sense now. Lance wasn't an ingenious gambler by night after all. He was just a contented employee who got his share of tips *because of his work ethic and decency*.

"Now comes *my* question," said Lance.

George repositioned himself in the chair and gave his undivided attention. "Shoot," he ordered in a friendly tone.

"You and I know that it's always the Lord who guides us to good fortune," he pointed out. "When I was hired on at the casino, things began to go my way all of a sudden." George was impressed and wanted to hear more. "They didn't have to train me much as a shuttle driver because I know this town. I also get called on to assist in the hotel; which is something I just love to do."

"Your tips must be enormous," commented George.

Looking at his feet, the modest servant spoke in a soft voice. "Well, they can be at times..." He then looked at George and began to share some trade secrets. "What I noticed is that the happier I am; the happier my passengers are. From there, they usually hand out what they can."

George saw the beauty in what was said and probed deeper. "That's brilliant! Where did you learn that from, anyway?"

It was now Lance's turn. Looking directly at the man who had once sponsored him in the name of the Lord, he prepared to give his answer. Pointing at George he said with conviction, "I learned that from *you*."

A perplexed expression covered George's face. *"Me?"* he questioned.

"Yes, *you!*" confirmed Lance Henry Wadsworth. "That night when you accepted me at the fellowship, I shared my happiness with you. I told you that I felt like I just won a contest. You explained to me that I did, and that it was a *happiness contest*. You told me that everyone won that night, especially God!"

Lance took a breath to gather himself. "I looked to the sky and thanked the Lord for what I found when that casino hired me. All the while, I could only think of you and what you've done for my

life. It then occurred to me what a great fit you'd be with us."
Looking at his fellowship brother, he addressed him. "They are
looking for another driver who would fill in the gaps throughout
the casino when needed. They also want a doorman. One who
would be considered a dignified senior. I told them that I knew of
the perfect candidate who could drive for us, and that I'd ask."

The man looking for a job with benefits and a retirement tensed
up.

"They are interested in you and promised not to post the opening
until you are contacted first," he informed. Pointing at George, he
stressed his point a little further. "Look, I know that you already
have a good career in another field. Something compelled me to
stop the works regardless - and get you in line first."

George felt an epiphany with the realization that the prayer he'd
cast earlier that day had already been answered! All over a lost
soul who had attended a fellowship meeting long ago. George
Willis Freeman stood up and extended his hand. "You have found
your man!" he exclaimed.

Chapter IX

GEORGE PASSED HIS INTERVIEW with flying colors.

It was Lance Wadsworth himself who trained him on both the shuttle job and the fundamentals of the hotel. A few tidbits about the casino in general were also thrown in.

George noticed something that served as testimony to the former auto mechanic's faith. The man had a hidden cup in the driver's compartment for tithing. When time allowed, he would access the two jars, making sure that at least ten percent would make it to the spare one with a cross on it. "It doesn't have to stop here," explained the trainer. "There are many worthy causes in this town that could always use a little help," he added. *George felt he was at the fellowship and learning from Lance.*

The instructor would constantly encourage his recruit by saying, "You're gonna be an all-star around here!"

The hotel venture was a world of its own. There were times when the duo rotated driving chores with another driver and assisted as bellhops. It was the same 'happiness contest' all over again. The extra effort, laced with genuine hospitality and charming smiles, always equated to more gratuities.

"George," whispered Lance as a limousine pulled up. "Once you get their stuff in their room, remember to offer getting ice for them. It works wonders!"

"Thanks," he whispered back. "I'll remember that."

Within two days, the new hire was cut loose and on his own.

The result?

Within the opening minutes of flying solo, Lance saw George's first customer give him an extended handshake. He saw his gracious co-worker apply a warm handshake – with the sudden realization that there was something in his customer's hand *being transferred to his*.

George Willis Freeman smiled at the friendly man who was entering the casino and waved. Next he looked down and saw that a ten-dollar bill was placed in his hand. At that moment it dawned on the new employee how much he was appreciated. A patron had just gifted him for caring about those he served- and he loved it!

Lance approached George and said, "What did I tell ya!" He shook George's hand and congratulated him. Next, he asked if he could look at the tip. George willfully handed it to him as a customer entered the shuttle. "Got to go!" cried out the new driver.

There was a reason why Lance wanted to see George's first tip. The following day he presented him a small gift neatly wrapped. George almost cried when he opened it. His first tip was framed identically to the one in Lance's living room.

George loved his new job and added his personal touch, *just as Lance Wadsworth did*. He would even safely park his vehicle to assist the elders who needed help boarding and getting off. It was common for him to have shifts where his tip jar had to be emptied early to create more room.

The certified accountant was well aware of the tax laws. He sat down with a calculator and estimated his new income after taxes were taken out. This would include his tips. To his surprise, he was already making quite a bit more than at his old job. George was also in an environment that brought him far more happiness. He was especially pleased that he could now match the generous donations Lance was giving to their church.

***

It was a week into the job when George decided to tell his family. It started off with a surprise. "Tonight we have a dinner engagement at a place you've never been before," he announced.

The household was ecstatic!

"Well, what prompted this?" asked his wife.

"You'll find out!" came the response.

He drove his family to the lavish casino that the whole world seemed to know about. From there, the newest employee took them inside to the popular Italian restaurant. It was at that table when he explained that his job of twenty years had gone out of business.

"What are you going to do, dad?" asked a concerned Junior.

"You're surrounded by it," he replied. "I got hired on here a week ago, and I love it!" he exclaimed. "This is the best place a guy could ever work," he added.

At once his wife and two children got out of their seats and hugged their hero. "We're so proud of you!" said Crystal.

Dinner was a hit. Later George gave his family a tour of the casino. "Wow!" cried out Mary Jane as she took in the colorful lights and beautiful music. "This place is awesome!"

Later that night, Crystal gave praise to her husband for coming through for the family once again. She then said something that would later haunt him.

"I just hope that your old boss, Mr. Tucker, is okay."

Chapter X

GEORGE FELL ASLEEP THINKING ABOUT HIS FORMER BOSS. He knew deep inside that his callous image was just a ruse. For whatever reason, it was outwardly projected in life to hide the inner man he really was. A man who was secretively compassionate and just as vulnerable as the rest of us.

George's new schedule gave him the following day off. He would get up early and make breakfast for the family. From there, he would wash the dishes as the family embarked on their priorities. "Great job, Dad!" called out Junior.

George was sitting at the dining room table enjoying a cup of coffee. Again and again, thoughts of his former boss had crossed his mind. Finally, George set his coffee down and bowed his head. In prayer, he asked the Lord to enhance the welfare of his former boss. To bring him peace, and to place him in an even better situation, like the very one he was just blessed with. He then volunteered to be a soldier who would assist in any way.

Soon he had a flashback about the talk he had with Lance and the job opportunities he'd spoken of. It was emphasized that the casino was looking for another driver *and a dignified senior to serve as a doorman.*

Immediately, George got on the phone and contacted his supervisor. "Hey!" he exclaimed. "I think I've got the perfect guy to be the casino's next doorman. And believe me, this senior is very dignified!"

"That sounds great, George! We'll hold off on the interviews and see what your man has to say to all of this."

Within half an hour, George was driving in front of his old office. The building seemed to be empty, but he could see that Mr. Tucker's office light was still on. *That old goat would never leave a light on. The electricity bill would keep him up for months!* the former employee said to himself.

To his delight, the front door was open. He took the elevator to the top floor and walked to the former president's office. Tapping on the door, he heard, "Come on in, Freeman."

George was astonished by the quick, accurate response. He entered the room with the sweeping view of the countryside. There, sitting behind his desk, was Benjamin Miles Tucker IV cool, calm, and collected. It were as if it was just another day of business. "How did you know it was me?" asked George.

"You're the only one who's ever cared about me," came the casual reply.

"Mind if I take a seat and visit with you for a while?" he asked.

"Not at all," said the old-timer. "We're not in any hurry today."

George detected an ounce of humor and appreciated it. From there, he initiated a conversation. "So what are your plans now?" he asked.

"Plans for what?" he barked back. "I've never had a family of my own. It's just me and the taxman."

"Can I share something with you?" he asked.

"Go ahead, Freeman."

George began to tell him about his new job and how much he liked it. "I was always grateful to work for you," he pointed out.

"I understand that, Freeman. Continue," said the man in the expensive suit.

George covered on how much fun the casino was and about the tips he received. "People handing out money because you're doing your job right? I like that!" he commented.

Benefits like medical, vision, dental, and employee discounts for the fine restaurants were mentioned. "Benefits? What's that?" he asked facetiously. "It was my employees who got them. I could never afford to cover myself."

George told him about the doorman position. "You will still be wearing a suit, and there will be those who hand you tips!" he added.

"All that for opening a door for them, before they lose their money?" he asked with a puzzled look. "I think I'd like a job like that."

George was astounded at how amenable his usually distant former employer was. "That's great!" he said. "That is, if you don't mind working with me again."

"That will be the best part of it," he replied in a fatherly tone.

George gave him the number to call and left the ball in his court.

"Thank you, Freeman," was returned.

"The pleasure's mine," said George as he left with a skip to his walk.

George

***

It was apparent that Benjamin Willis Tucker IV was the right man for the new position. He showed up early every shift and formally stood at his post. George would often see a friendly exchange taking place between his old boss and a customer. At times he would see a monetary reward of respect handed to him. There was also a lot of good talk about the new doorman circulating about. It was obvious that Benjamin Tucker liked his new job.

There was still something eluding the former accountant. How come his former employer would still never give *him* a smile? For George Freeman, a smile from him would be far more meaningful than what any slot could generate.

George studied the man he once worked for and noticed how he was loosening up with life. He even became friends with Lance and joked around with him. Still, he only got an impersonation of a cigar-store Indian from Mr. Tucker.

One day, it happened. George was giving Lance the keys to the shuttle so that he could service the hotel for the remainder of his shift. It was at that time when none other than Benjamin Tucker himself tipped his hat and opened the door for him. Once inside, the old man called out, "Hey Freeman, this is what a tip looks like!" George turned around and saw the new doorman proudly display *his* framed first tip. It was a crisp twenty-dollar bill that Lance had obviously enshrined for him. The dignified senior then offered some free advice. "And don't forget the ice!"

What happened next made George's day. Benjamin gave him a Cheshire grin followed by a thumbs-up!

It was official: they were now buds on the job!

The shuttle driver could only shake his head in disbelief. George was now laughing out loud and fired a thumbs-up right back.

While walking to his next post, he suddenly realized where he was, and what had just happened. He was in the very casino where he had challenged his dreams not too long ago. Dreams about fancy vehicles and riches; but not about his fellow man *or the Lord*.

It had dawned on the man of faith that it only took the power of prayer to get him what he really needed. He not only got a much better job at a place he loved; but he'd also played a role in enhancing the lives of two men he greatly respected. To make things even better, he got to work with them in the funnest place - ever!

Finally, he got the satisfaction of seeing something that had eluded him for two decades. He'd finally lived long enough to see Mr. Benjamin Miles Tucker IV flowing with so much joy, that he couldn't contain it any longer.

The desperate man who initially challenged the neighborhood casino to find his fortune got more than what he bargained for. With devout faith and the power of prayer, George had surpassed any prize ever won in a casino. He even went beyond what a winning lottery ticket could bring.

On this special day, George Willis Freeman had placed *first* in the happiness contest!

The End

Cocoa The Bear

Introduction

TEDDY DOWNING WALKED DOWN THE LAVISH HALLWAY with forest green carpet and beige walls. Amazingly, this thirteen-year-old who never knew his biological parents displayed an amazing amount of maturity.

The slightly overweight boy with soft brown hair parted to one side and matching brown eyes took notice of the beautiful artwork. Meticulously, he digested each and every display that graced the corridor with oak molding. Teddy loved this part of his day. Such walks, whether through a retirement community or a public building, always brought forth a spectacle that sent a message all its own.

In time, the visitor reached a door decorated with paper flowers, along with a replica of the American flag placed under the peephole. It was room 124, where one spunky Mrs. Clark lived.

Teddy Lee Downing was on a mission. The eighth grader from the local elementary school had volunteered himself for Senior Citizen Duty. This was a good cause he'd initially learned about when his class visited that very retirement home not long ago.

Equipped with his patented smile and a fresh batch of cookies, Teddy knocked on the door. Immediately, it was opened by an enthused Mrs. Clark. The spunky eighty-five-year-old who was leaning against her walker greeted Teddy. "Right on time!" she exclaimed. "Come on in, Teddy. It's so good to see you!"

"It's nice to see you too, Mrs. Clark," came the cheerful reply.

Gretta Anna Clark got lucky. Where she lived, very few dropped by to visit. Despite various efforts to passionately reach out to the community, it appeared that Teddy was one of the very few to respond. He was also the only student to step forward.

The frisky senior remembered the day Teddy first set foot in the complex. "We knew you'd come through for us!" she'd often say.

"My grandmother and I baked some chocolate chip cookies," said the boy, who came well-prepared.

"Oh, that's wonderful!" said the charming elder. "I'll make some tea."

It would be an understatement to say that Teddy Lee Downing had a heart of gold. He also had a keen eye for those who felt abandoned. After all, it was the very pain the unwanted child had felt throughout his entire life. Thank God for grandmothers.

School life was a mixed bag for the non-athletic honor student. The teachers loved Teddy, but his classmates generally had nothing to do with him. He just didn't fit in with the 'in crowd.' At times he was even bullied a bit.

There was a silver lining to one Teddy Lee Downing. At a young age, he was blessed with his faith and the power of forgiveness. That, along with holding true to his values, set him apart from the rest. He not only understood his peers; he seemed to have an understanding with the entire world.

And now our story begins...

Chapter I

TEDDY DOWNING WAS SITTING IN A CLASS that seemed to be drifting off into dreamland. The science teacher just out of college knew how to throw some kindling on the fire when such boredom overtook her students.

The twenty-five-year-old would liven things up by asking humorous questions designed to make everyone laugh. This tactic would in essence jump-start the entire class, thus getting them all on the same page once again. This tool was a little risky however. It could only work *if the right person was called upon.* It would have to be a proven student who was mature enough to understand *why.* Mrs. White needed to look no further than the star pupil in the front row: Teddy Downing.

In moments, Teddy responded to a peculiar question about 'a refrigerator running'. Knowingly, he bit the bait, causing an avalanche of laughter to ensue. The science teacher then gave a quick wink of thanks to her go-to guy. The comedy act worked like a charm! At once, all sat up and paid attention to her presentation.

Later, the teacher crossed paths when Teddy was alone and said, "You're such a godsend. You always do the right thing!"

Such heroics were indicative of Teddy Downing's character. He was also big enough of a person to laugh at himself, *but never at others*. Valor that often came at a price. There were those who despised the innocent overweight boy with the cherubic face. It was his image of being a role model who pulled good grades that often worked against him.

Case in point was one Randy Harris Ghering.

Randy was a ruggedly handsome classmate who towered over most. The teen with dark straight hair and matching eyes was also the school's prized athlete.

There was more.

He possessed a dash of rebellion laced with his own brand of humor. A combination that most girls found to be irresistible. He was clearly the most popular boy in school and was always invited to every party. Sadly, it would be Randy Ghering himself who would be Teddy's worst critic. Whenever Teddy showed respect to a teacher, Randy would often blurt out an insult.

That day was no different. Randy had to give Teddy a verbal jab under his breath for assisting Mrs. White's effort to rejuvenate the class. "Why don't you two get married, Dumpling?" Teddy shrugged off the verbal assault. He also pretended that the nickname 'Dumpling' didn't bother him.

***

Walking home from school often held an adventure for Teddy. In his travels, he would sometimes visit the fire department, the Senior Center, the library, or walk through the park. On such jaunts, it was always Cocoa who he would visit first.

Cocoa was an eight-year-old American black bear with cinnamon-like fur. Teddy first met the affectionate *Ursus americanus* on a Cub Scout retreat. The declawed yearling in a cage displayed a special interest in the adopted child. Despite wearing a muzzle,

Cocoa did all she could to lick the child who stood out. Teddy, in return, was allowed to hug and pet his new friend.

It was love at first sight!

After all, Teddy was fully aware that they both held something in common. Each was abandoned at a young age.

Through time, the bond between Cocoa and Teddy grew. In fact, the teen had taught the bear two tricks. One was to 'sit' upon command. The other was to shake hands just like Lassie. The once cuddly cub had matured into a 160-pound sow. Still, Teddy would feed carrots and other vegetation to the animal in captivity. On occasion, a keeper would allow Teddy to rub his muzzled friend between the ears and across her neck and back. Cocoa would in turn lean against her friend as if it were a cat purring.

***

Teddy Downing arrived home from school. "How was school today, Teddy?" asked his fifty-eight-year-old grandmother.

"Just fine, Grandma," replied the grandson. "I saw Cocoa today!" he exclaimed.

"I thought so," commented the stout, gray-haired woman in glasses.

Emily Marie Downing was always there for her grandson. When her renegade daughter couldn't cope with the trials and tribulations of adolescence, it was the mother herself who continued parenting. A labor of love from the unconditional love she always held for her grandchild.

Emily knew that her grandson had a rough time at school. The family budget restricted purchases to the local thrift store and yard sales. Poor Teddy could never afford the latest of fashions that would somewhat help in blending in with his peers. The boy almost never had the pocket change to get a burger or go to the movies. He was also timid and overly cautious due to the lack of a father figure.

There were days when *Dumpling* came home crying. He would tell his grandmother of the cruelty he had received that day in school, as well as on the playground. Emily would hug the man of the house and discuss the real reason he was brought into this world. "You are a soldier of God; you were brought here to lead others."

It was just Teddy and his grandmother, surviving life together, and they loved it! When he wasn't picked to be on anyone's team, visiting older members in the community would suffice. Above all, there was always church, his grandmother, and Cocoa...

Chapter II

EMILY DOWNING ENTERED THE CHURCH'S BANQUET ROOM WITH a warm container. This was the Downings' contribution to the weekly potluck. A bag of outdated frozen vegetables, steamed and ready to eat. The charitable contribution from the local food bank was going from Peter to Paul one last time.

These evenings meant everything to the family of two. It was a midweek social event evolving around lessons from the Good Book. For Teddy, the highlight was when Pastor Morris would give an inspirational talk. It was such guidance, conducted by the man who was always there for the fatherless boy, that left a huge impression.

That night's message was about how our Lord sends us signs through what others say. Including from our enemies. Every word spoken by the pastor left an impact. The youth would continue his life paying closer attention to what others had to say. He now understood to search for the hidden messages sent by the Lord Himself. Clues that needed to be spiritually deciphered to help better serve.

A fellowship feast would follow. In true form, Emily and her grandson would always be last in line. Usually there would be enough casserole, salad, and buttered bread to fill their plates. By the end of the evening, every tray would be scraped clean.

This particular evening, Pastor Morris called out to the parishioners. The tall, pleasant man with conservative blond hair and blue eyes spoke. "We're due to have a fundraiser," the angelical man announced.
"If anyone has any ideas, please contact me."

That night Teddy reflected on his evening. He loved the sermon that Pastor Morris gave and those he visited with. He then thought about his request. There was something about his plea that seemed to reach out to him specifically. *We're due to have a fundraiser...*

It was as if he were being singled out by the Lord Himself.

***

The next day, Teddy was informed about an art fair being coordinated. "We have so much around here that we might as well display it to the community," explained Mrs. Winfield.

After school, he attended his Boy Scout meeting. "We need more community involvement," said Scout Leader Roy Hensen. "Let's see what we can do to for our neighbors."

Later, the boy in uniform dropped by to visit Cocoa on the way home. It was feeding time, with none other than Teddy Downing himself given the honor to feed his fury friend. "Cocoa certainly loves you," commented Karen Fulton. She then said something he'd heard from other volunteers. "This zoo could certainly use more people like you."

Her comment registered deeply. It began to intertwine with the messages that his grandmother, Pastor Morris, scout leader, teachers, friends at the Senior Center, and zoo personnel had pitched.

Something inside Teddy's soul was brewing...

***

Teddy and his grandmother were enjoying a family night. This consisted of hot cider, popcorn, and watching television. It was a carnival bringing happiness to thousands that caught their eye that evening.

In Teddy's mind, he kept playing back the comments that appeared to be directed at him:

We knew you'd come through for us...

You are a soldier of God; you were brought here to lead others...

You're such a godsend. You always do the right thing...

We're due to have a fundraiser...

We have so much around here that we might as well display it to the community...

Let's see what we can do for our neighbors...

This zoo could certainly use more people like you...

***

Teddy woke up the next day in a whirlwind of thought. He kept thinking of the many who had addressed him lately. It was as if he were to decode an important message sent from a higher power.

How right he was. That day, a few more clues would be sent.

In school, Randy Ghering was inviting friends to his family's cabin for a campout.
"Dumpling can't go unless he brings a bear to play with." Immense laughter ensued.

Teddy wanted to be accepted. He also wanted to be included on the campout and did his best to hide the pain.

At the zoo, a volunteer said, "It's too bad you can't take Cocoa out to the forest and play with her."

It was at the Senior Center when it all came together. It was ninety-two-year-old Mr. Stratton driving in the final stake. "When I was your age, our entire town would get everything it had together and throw a carnival. They would bring in animals from the zoo, sell food, have games and contests. It was fun for everybody, and it brought in a lot of money."

The final piece of the puzzle had been placed on Teddy's lap. His soul was now replaying the latest set of clues sent to him.

Dumpling can't go unless he brings a bear to play with...

It's too bad you can't take Cocoa out to the forest and play with her...

When I was your age, our entire town would get everything it had together and throw a carnival. They would bring in animals from the zoo, sell food, have games and contests. It was fun for everybody, and it brought in a lot of money...

Teddy Lee Downing finally got it! Wasting no time, he raced home to share *his idea* with his grandmother. "Oh, what a lovely idea!" she exclaimed. "I'm sure Pastor Morris would like it."

Chapter III

THE IRON WAS HOT with some daylight hours remaining. A call was made, and soon the Downings were sitting in church with Pastor Morris. The reverent man was elated over *Teddy's idea*. "Marvelous!" he praised. "Just marvelous..."

"We can sell hotdogs and soda pop," Teddy pointed out. "My school even has artwork that can be displayed!"

It was understood that such an undertaking would involve many. More calls were made, and soon a broad range of approval was received. Teddy's Boy Scout troop was excited to get involved with such a charitable event. The school district volunteered, as did the Senior Center. The Park Department got into the act by designating a local campground to host the event. The word spread like wildfire with more and more reputable organizations stepping in.

Most importantly, it was Teddy himself who personally made the call to the local zoo. It was confirmed that Cocoa the bear, along with a few other exhibits, would be booked for this event. By the end of the week, all of the participants were accounted for and on the same page. It was universally agreed that the proceeds would go to the local church. The extravaganza was to take place the first weekend of the following month.

***

The town was in a frenzy preparing for the event. Even various clubs from neighboring towns volunteered their services. That week, Teddy received a merit badge at his Scout meeting for community service. It was followed by a standing ovation, along with an overtone of jealousy from one fellow member: Randy Ghering.

***

Teddy visited the Senior Center as a celebrity. The compassionate teen had made the local newspaper, to the delight of all. He was commended for his many charitable contributions ranging from litter patrol to running errands for the elders.

"We love you, Teddy!" cried out eighty-eight-year-old Suzanne Brighton. "You came up with something that will include all of us!"

Later, Teddy was visiting Cocoa. Upon sight, the crafty animal slid its nose into a nearby muzzle. It was Pavlov's Theory at its finest! In moments, the lonely bear was receiving the much-needed love she had been waiting for since their last visit. "Sit!" instructed the playmate. "Shake," projected a warm, encouraging tone. The two embraced as an on-duty veterinarian held the sow's leash with a watchful eye.

Cocoa's day was now complete, and so was Teddy's.

Chapter IV

The big day had finally arrived!

Parking lots were filling up early for the widely publicized spectacle. A roller coaster along with motorized go karts, a carousel, tall slides, and a Ferris wheel were just some of the rides waiting to be ventured. Booths were set up to sell hotdogs and other refreshments. Vendors were selling their products at discount prices.

There was more.

The local zoo brought in ponies for children to ride. They also brought in what would prove to be the star of the ball: Cocoa the bear!

Ingeniously, the zoo officials volunteered to have Teddy dressed in a safari outfit equipped with matching hat. His duty was to safely assist those who wanted to pose with the local celebrity. Teddy would comfort the muzzled star on a leash with able assistance nearby.

The cost? Four bits! It was an event full of amusement and novelties that had something for everybody.

***

That day, Teddy and Cocoa were the talk of the town. It seemed that everyone attending got their picture taken with the now famous black bear and her sidekick. It was practically becoming a fad!

In time, there was a lull in the action that one Randy Harris Ghering was waiting for. Teddy was sitting peacefully with the restricted bear. Immediately, the bully made his presence known by throwing a crunched-up candy wrapper at Teddy. It bounced off his shoulder and startled both Teddy and Cocoa.

Randy then began to make faces at the caged animal, followed by sporadic hand movements and howling noises. The mother bear was further enticed and started to growl. The tethered Cocoa tried to protect her family, but couldn't lunge forward.

Teddy petted her back and said, "Quit teasing her!"

Randy was in his glory and laughingly said, "You'll never be a man, Dumpling!" Satisfied, he left feeling in control.

***

Nightfall came quickly with a community bonfire becoming the focal point. There were still thousands attending who simply didn't want to go home. It was Teddy's first break in the day, and he had the honor of sitting next to Pastor Morris. "Brother Teddy," said the clergyman in a warm tone. "The Lord has certainly blessed us through you!" The fatherless boy seemed to be emotionally preoccupied. It was as if something were wrong. "What's wrong?" asked the pastor.

It took a while for the distraught teen to open up. Finally, he shared what Randy Ghering had done to Cocoa. "He's always trying to pick a fight with me and says that I'm not a man."

"You are definitely a man," assured Pastor Morris. "Randy is still immature enough not to see the grace in you. Stay strong," he advised. "There is a reason why Randy always takes notice of you." Leaning back, the wise man gave more advice. "Keep on praying; the Lord will set the stage when the time is right..."

Teddy did just that.

All at once, a woman's scream could be heard followed by a crashing sound. Everyone turned to see where the commotion was coming from. What they saw was a full-grown black bear eating food from a picnic table that was knocked over.

Cocoa had gotten out!

The showpiece who was in for the night had somehow escaped. The omnivorous creature was now tasting meat for the first time - and loved it. Suddenly, the bear stood on her hind legs and roared at her home range. It was a loud, echoing rumble that emphasized strength. All present were petrified with fear as Cocoa played catch-up with nature.

The bear started to twitch her nose, as if it detected something. She soon honed in on the predator she was in search of. The scorned female had business to attend.

Teddy ran to the empty cage and returned with Cocoa's muzzle. He arrived just in time to see Randy's back against a tree. The rival in wet clothing was staring eye-to-eye with a growling, full-grown bear. With confidence, Teddy approached Cocoa and called out her name.

"Cocoa..."

The American black bear stayed focused on her prey, as if Teddy wasn't there.

A second attempt was made with more authority. "Cocoa!"

The distracted bear turned to the familiar voice. Eye contact was established with the wild animal, but she didn't seem to recognize him.

All eyes were on the boy in the safari hat. "Sit," barked the master. Immediately, Cocoa did just that! Next he affectionately said, "Shake." The attentive bear extended her right paw as her playmate shook it. Without any resistance, *Dumpling* was allowed to secure the muzzle on Cocoa and walk her back to the open cage. Once inside, the boy who was always teased for never standing up for himself spent a few minutes alone with his friend.

Everyone knew that it's every animal's dream to be free. The same held true for Cocoa the bear, *unless a better life could be found.* After all, what all-American black bear could resist being rubbed on the back of its neck and being hugged? To be loved and fed almost every day by its most favorite human *ever!* If Cocoa were a dog, her tail would be wagging profusely. Soon the star of the day stepped out of the cage and assured that all was secured. "Good night, Cocoa," said the hero.

All who were present watched in astonishment, including a few of Teddy's classmates. What they witnessed was an act of bravery unsurpassed by any. Teddy noticed Pastor Morris giving him a smile of approval. The boy then gave a wave to the man who had mentored him. Immediately, the pastor waved back. It was then when the pastor's fatherly advice began to play back in his head:

Keep on praying; the Lord will set the stage when the time is right...

Teddy did just that. He prayed for his classmate, Randy Ghering. He then thanked Him for Cocoa being safe without anyone getting hurt.

It worked like a charm! At that very moment, none other than Randy Harris Ghering came running toward him. "Teddy, thank you so much!" he said while catching his breath. "That was so cool how you handled Cocoa!" It was Randy who extended a hand to shake Teddy's. A friendship was born!

It was a freshly forged bond based on prayer, respect, and appreciation. One that included an invitation to Randy's upcoming campout!

The End

The Old Man

Introduction

WILFRED BARTHOLOMEW PENNINGTON was a contented, mild-mannered man who lived alone. The frisky eighty-two-year-old with a full head of gray hair seemed to have a skip to his walk. That, along with his striking steel blue eyes and gracious smile, made him all the more dignified. The man also showed a lot of class by greeting any and all who crossed his path. His charm, accommodated with a sense of humor, made him a favorite in the neighborhood.

It would be an understatement to say that the retired postal clerk was loved by many. He was also that proverbial 'wise old man' whom troubled youth would seek for advice. On occasion there would be a lemonade-listening session on his front porch. Mr. Pennington truly cared for others and knew how to keep a secret *if it were kosher*.

It was known that this respected soul had acquired much wisdom from being a public servant. He also had years of Little League coaching and judging debate teams that sweetened the pot. His diplomacy was impeccable.

The day came when some local teens asked the reverent man for a special favor. One that their parents would absolutely object to. It was time for Wilfred Bartholomew Pennington to show that he still had it.

And now our story begins...

Chapter I

IT WAS A DAY LIKE ANY OTHER DAY when Wilfred Pennington stepped out of his front door. Rain or shine, the happy-go-lucky soul greeted every day as if it were Christmas.

Wilfred's morning stroll was just underway when he noticed two tall, husky boys approaching him. Squinting through his wire-rimmed glasses, he immediately recognized the teenagers with short brown hair and brown eyes. "Well, if it isn't the Bronson boys!" he exclaimed to the pair who could pass for twins. "I haven't seen you two in quite some time. How have you been?"

"Good morning, Mr. Pennington," greeted seventeen-year-old Bart.

"Hi, Mr. Pennington," said his younger brother, Noel.

"I can't believe how big you boys have gotten!" commented the man in the gray suit. "You're both beginning to look like your dad."

The brothers looked at one another as if they felt uncomfortable. Wilfred Pennington pretended not to notice. Finally Bart looked at Mr. Pennington and said, "We were actually going to visit you at your home."

"Visit me at my home?" questioned the old man. "Why, that would be wonderful! You are always welcome in my home."

Noel picked up where his brother left off. "We were going to ask you for a favor."

The elder's face contorted as he prepared for the worst. "A favor?" asked the inquisitive man.

The boys began to stutter as they looked down at the pavement. A moment of silence took place. Finally, Bart looked directly at Mr. Pennington and told him how 'cool' he was. Wilfred remained motionless and waited for the punchline. Bart then asked if he would buy some beer for him and his friends, for a party they were going to. "We have the money for it," he said.

All eyes were on Mr. Pennington as he digested the request. Suspense was mounting as the brothers waited for their answer. It came.

"Ah, a Ruben sandwich," came the reply. "Why, it's been almost a year since I last had one of those!" he said.

Bart and Noel looked at one another, dumbfounded. Next, they turned their heads at an angle and stared back at their subject with open mouths. They simply didn't understand the answer they'd just heard.

"A Ruben sandwich?" asked Noel in a high-pitched tone.

"Yes," replied the old man. "A Ruben sandwich, and it will be at Holly's Cafe. They're the best in town!" he emphasized. There was a pause in the retiree's thought process as he seemed to correct himself. "Wait a minute," he said while touching his chin. Pointing at the brothers he proclaimed, "The Evergreen Restaurant gives them a run for the money. They have a salad bar with their own homemade bread and butter," he stated. "Why, a guy could stay there all day for under ten dollars!" he chuckled.

Bart and Noel were at a loss for words as the old man continued. "Their coffee wins awards every year, and it's always fresh." Another pause took place as he gave the matter a little more thought.

The teens remained quiet.

"Wait, wait, wait," he said in a muffled tone. "Holly's also has great, freshly brewed coffee."

"No," he resumed. "I have to go with Holly's. They're a little more spendy, but definitely worth it!" he defended while shaking a finger.

His audience remained silent.

Just then, the old man's memory festered out more information that had to be shared. He seemed to be getting more and more excited as he pointed at the duo. "Their homemade preserves always get the blue ribbons at every county fair!" he cried out. There was another slight pause as the aging man gained his composure. "I realize that you two might be a bit too young to appreciate that; but you certainly will when you get older."

Bart fired back with a direct comment. "We came here to see if you'd buy us some beer."

"I heard that," replied Mr. Pennington in a firm voice. "I now have to tell your father about this."

Chapter II

THE BROTHERS FELT BETRAYED by the neighbor who'd watched them grow up.

"We thought you were *cool*!" Noel cried out.

"Why, I believe that I still am," answered the old man with a smug expression.

"Please don't tell our dad!" pleaded Bart. "He'd get mad at us..."

"He won't stay mad for very long," predicted the old man. "That is, if you tell him before I do." Mr. Wilfred Bartholomew Pennington had more to say. "He'll let off a little steam at first. He would then start to think about things and gather himself. In essence, he'd realize that you two respected him so much that you told him about this, regardless of any consequences. That right there will mean everything to him! It will make him all the more proud of his sons." The wise old man threw in a little extra.

"If I'm the one who tells him first, it will be different. He won't be mad; he'll be disappointed and hurt. He'll probably say very little and leave with his tail between his legs." Wilfred then added a finishing touch. "He'll just be a broken man who used to be someone. A hollow shell..."

The old man then pointed out some attributes about their dad. "If he were to get mad, it would only be toward a person who was harmful to others *and knew better.*" The man approaching his nineties reflected on past memories. "I would certainly pity the fool who did," he said under his breath.

Looking at the brothers, the old man continued. "You guys know about your father's football career, don't you?" The boys beamed with pride as they nodded. Mr. Pennington became animated as he shared a few stories.

"Why, I remember this one play when a poor runningback was like a deer in the headlights! He saw your old man coming and froze. Your dad had class and gently set him down on the turf."

The Bronson boys loved what they were hearing and wanted more!

"There was this one time when he blasted through two linemen to get to the quarterback. Luckily, that player was close enough to the sidelines to save his neck!

Bart and Noel laughed in approval.

"I've watched him intercept passes where no one would tackle him."

A few more heroic stories were shared about their father's dazzling football career. In time, Mr. Pennington brought the conversation up to the present. "Your dad played those games for all of us. He's the sole reason why we made it to the state playoffs every year when he was playing." Looking at the sons he added, "And he still fights for this community!"

"Please don't tell on us, Mr. Pennington," gasped Bart in desperation.

"Look," said the old man. "He's going to love you guys even more because you knew to go to him. He'll practically cry when you show him that you can tell him anything. From there, he will probably share a few embarrassing escapades he was involved in when he was your age. It's all good."

The old man then stressed a point. "It's the poor guy who questions the bond he has with his sons who's gonna get it! That is, if he actually has a bond with his sons..."

Bart and Noel looked at each other, realizing that they were failing their beloved father.

At that moment, the senior on Medicare reached into his pocket and pulled out a prescription. He opened it and pulled out the cotton saying, "Oh, good. I'll be needing this for my ears."

Next, he looked at his watch. "Let's see; I should make it to your dad's place in about twenty minutes." In a humorous tone, he looked at the boys and chuckled, "There was a day when I was the fastest kid on the block."

With cotton in place, the old man started to walk up the street. Without any hesitation, Bart and Noel ran.

Chapter III

"WHAT?" CRIED OUT FORTY-TWO-YEAR-OLD MERLE BRONSON. "Did I hear you guys right?"

Bart and his brother remained quiet. Wisely, they had followed old man Pennington's advice and were facing round one. "My own sons?" cried out the former linebacker in disbelief.

The sons remained quiet.

The man who worked out several times a week paced around the living room. Suddenly, he calmed down with a faint smile crossing his face. "Let's sit down and talk about this," he calmly said.

The boys looked at each other, trying their best not to laugh. Through the wise old man, they knew what their father's next course of action would be.

Soon a teary-eyed dad was at the dinner table gazing at his sons. "You guys could have gotten away with something, but instead you told me," he said in admiration.

Immediately the emotional man leaned forward and hugged his boys. Sobbing, he said, "I love you guys so much."

From there, forgiveness was granted with confessions to follow. It turned out that their own sweet dad had a few skeletons of his own...

There were a few renegade stories about weekends and alcohol. Admissions about graffiti and pranks were also unveiled. Dad even admitted that he'd once shoplifted. "I'm no better than you guys," he explained. "It just took me a little longer to come around, that's all."

The boys were acquitted with Mr. Pennington to thank. It was at that time when Merle looked out the front window and saw the old man walking up the steps. Immediately, his defense mechanisms kicked into gear. *Why, that old fool; he's trying to get my boys into trouble,* he thought to himself. *I'll show him!*

Merle opened the door just as the neighbor was about to knock and yelled, "If it's about that beer thing, I've already been told!"

Wilfred Pennington knew that there was more venom to come and braced himself. Merle proceeded to blast the messenger with harsh facts. "Yes, they know that they did wrong, but they came clean with me; and it's all taken care of!" He then defended his sons further by giving them a little praise. "Did you forget that they are honor students and volunteer for our church?" The protector of the family did all he could to restrain himself and slammed the door in the old man's face. "There!" shouted Merle Bronson as he slapped his hands together.

Bart and his brother watched the verbal melee and felt guilty. After all, it was Mr. Pennington himself who'd masterminded a format that would get them pardoned. The boys knew that their loving dad was momentarily in a space where he couldn't look beyond his cherished sons. It would be later when he would come to his full senses.

That evening, Merle took his family out for dinner as a victory celebration. It was for having wonderful kids. Bart and Noel did not feel right that evening.

Chapter IV

THE NEXT DAY THE BRONSON BROTHERS GOT UP EARLY. It was in hope of crossing paths with the old man who took a walk every morning. True to form, Old Faithful was seen coming their way.

"Good morning, gentlemen!" greeted Mr. Pennington.

Immediately the teens apologized for the wrath their father had unloaded on him. "It's okay, fellas," he said laughingly. "He was just burning the lower forty; it gives you a better crop." He then raised his arms high in the air and proclaimed, "And today is harvest time!"

Bart and Noel were amazed by Mr. Pennington's outlook on life. The chipper old man continued, "Oh, this is gonna be good!" Leaning close to the brothers, he quietly said, "I even skipped last night's dinner for this."

The gracious man laughed to himself and said, "Now it's just a matter of time for your dad to see me. Trust me, he'll be looking for me today." Once again, he leaned close to the brothers and whispered, "I might even use an old trick and pretend to be tying my shoelaces when I'm in front of his place."

No truer words were spoken, because at that moment, a familiar masculine voice called out.

"Wilfred!" called out Merle. "I owe you an apology, brother." The old master remained silent and let Merle Bronson set the stage. "Hey, let's you and I step out and patch this mess up!"

"Sounds good to me," replied Wilfred.

"The Evergreen Restaurant is a nice place," suggested the man who now had an arm around Wilfred's shoulder.

"That's a nice place," replied the hungry soul.

"Wait!" said Merle. "This is a special outing. Let's make it Holly's instead!"

The lovable old man was now practically starving and seconded the motion. "Oh, I like that idea a lot!"

Together, the two neighbors let bygones be bygones and marched to the renowned dining establishment. The boys could hear their dad talking to Mr. Pennington as they grew distant. "You know, I've always liked you, Wilfred..."

The brothers watched the final chapter play out to perfection. Looking at each other, they felt rejuvenated. Both were in awe from what they had just experienced and began to feel good about themselves. A valuable lesson had been taught about respecting their parents and the elders around them.

A lesson they would always carry for the rest of their lives.

The End

Epilogue

THE FOUR STORIES YOU HAVE JUST READ serve as testimony to one's faith. Each setting presents the common scenario of how we humans often auspiciously (and inauspiciously) reach out to be accepted.

'The Cabin In The Woods' illustrates how the Lord provides for us long before we take notice. Our Heavenly Father uses various forms of His creation to guide us while we slip and slide through our trials. In the end, we realize that He was there the whole time. We also learn that long ago, He delivered what was most crucial.

In the story, 'George', we have a good church-going family man whose life is going through a spiritual change; all unbeknownst to himself. In the end, it was the needs of his fellow man that were actually being addressed, with our star answering the calling!

In 'Cocoa The Bear,' it was a crusading thirteen-year-old Teddy Downing who was forever setting a good example for us all. Despite continuous rejection from many of his peers, the boy's unconditional love for his fellow man (and bear) would prevail in the end! It was all about how diligently he served others while never compromising his values. It was Teddy himself who drew the attention of others and got them into the game. The class bully, and even Cocoa the bear served as prime examples.

'The Old Man' covers how sometimes youth can stray a bit, regardless of one's background. It was the old man himself who taught a valuable lesson by updating the concept of free will. Wilfred Bartholomew Pennington himself laid the cards down, face-up. Using his years of wisdom, he let the Bronson brothers correct the mistake they were in the process of making, all on their own. A method that further secured a family bond and a neighborhood friendship.

In each story, it was clearly a spiritual path set by our Lord that needed to be followed. Decisions that we all face at one time or another in this acid test known as life.

Thank you, and may God bless!

Matt Shea

About the Author

MATT SHEA IS A DEVELOPING AUTHOR having published nine paperbacks and thirteen ebooks. He is greatly inspired by the writings of Andy Griffith and focuses on the common folk that small towns are made of.

Matt Shea with his daughter, Laura.

He credits the success of his first book, *The Groundskeeper And Other Short Stories* to his family. The values that were instilled throughout his childhood gave him the strong sense of justice that is conveyed throughout his writings. The Shea family is only an average American family from an average neighborhood. Their secret is that they are close knit and accept others.

Matt's mother, Vyerl set an example of being self-sacrificing; having never placed herself first. She always cared about the feelings of others, no matter who they were. She even sponsored many foster children despite having a family of eight. During the holidays, the Roman Catholic mom had been known to have a Hanukkah bush for their Jewish friends. There were even years when the family would make Christmas gifts and personally deliver them to seniors in rest homes.

Many of Matt's friends are senior citizens or foreign born. He has the common practice of brewing a pot of tea and inviting them over to watch Alfred Hitchcock Presents. Together they will watch Alfred, share a cup of tea, and afterwords listen to his manuscripts. Sometimes these social gatherings last well beyond midnight.

"This is where I get most of my ideas," says Matt. "I learned this from my mom."

Matt Shea appreciates all who take the time to read his stories. He even has a site with a free 'family friendly' audiobook along with some stories in their entirety thrown in! This author also extends his website and email address for those who have any comments or ideas. Matt knows that through other people, he can expand as a writer and a person.

Matt Shea
www.mattsheabooks.net
www.worknmatt7@aol.com

Books by Matt Shea

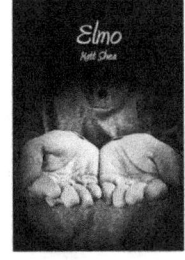

More Uplifting
Stories From
Matt Shea Books!

Matt Shea